DODGE

ML NYSTROM

HOT TREE PUBLISHING

DODGE

DRAGON RUNNERS MC
BOOK 6

ML NYSTROM

HOT TREE PUBLISHING

DRAGON RUNNERS MC

MUTE

STUD

BLUE

TABLE

BRICK

DODGE

MACATEER BROTHERS

RUN WITH IT

READY FOR IT

HOLD IT CLOSE

RISK IT ALL

GIVE IT TO ME

THE DUTCHMEN MC

THE PRICE OF REDEMPTION

THE PRICE OF FORGIVENESS

THE PRICE OF PEACE

THE PRICE OF ATONEMENT

For information, contact the publisher, Hot Tree Publishing.

WWW.HOTTREEPUBLISHING.COM

EDITING: HOT TREE EDITING

COVER DESIGNER: BOOKSMITH DESIGN

E-BOOK ISBN: 978-1-922679-74-1

PAPERBACK ISBN: 978-1-922679-75-8

CHAPTER 1

I DIDN'T WANT TO MOVE. MY HEAD POUNDED, AND MY mouth tasted like garbage disposal fodder. Shards of bright light pierced my brain when I tried to open my eyes, so I squeezed them shut with a gurgled groan and burrowed into the pillow.

Then shock number one zapped through my brain.

An arm lay around my waist, holding me against a body. A warm body. A male body. A *naked* male body. This was odd, as Chase didn't cuddle. Ever.

The totally unfamiliar sensation was enough to make me come awake with a mental jerk. I forced my eyes open and painfully squinted around the strange room.

Hotel. Luxury from the looks of the furniture. My

hotel? I'd never been in the rooms, only the kitchens where I worked as a sous chef.

The man behind me grunted and stretched. Yep, he was definitely naked, as the morning wood at my back showed. My eyes zeroed in on the little happy pile of clothes neatly laid over one of the big, soft easy chairs. My clothes. *Shit.*

Second shock: I was naked too.

Where the fuck am I, and what the hell have I done?

The man pushed the ratted tangle my hair had become off my neck and growled in a just-woke-up voice, "Mornin', sweetness. I 'spect your head isn't feelin' all that great right now."

My heart rate turned the speed up to puree. I didn't move, but I grunted an affirmation.

"Stay here. There are some complimentary painkillers in the bathroom. I'll get 'em for you."

He kissed me lightly, and the bed shifted as he left it. I rolled over and got a full view of his beefy ass as he sauntered across the room. *Damn, that is fine!* He had a back tattoo of what looked like a dragon in full flight. Gold and green with wings spread over a twisting path of flames. *Game of Thrones* fan? He would have made a nice Khal Drogo, except his hair was short and blond.

What am I doing?

I lifted the thick comforter and glanced down at my body, confirming my naked state and getting my third shock: my pussy was shaved. There was no doubt I'd been intimate with this strange man; the damning evidence sat before my eyes. Blood rushed through my head as vessels burst while I dug through my vague memories of the night before.

"Went down on you twice, but we didn't have sex, if that's what you're wonderin'."

I whipped the comforter down and clutched it to my breasts. "I just… I…."

What the hell are you supposed to say in these situations? It's not like I've had a lot of experience waking up in a hotel room with a stranger. Like never. Fuck!

He stood by the bed, a packet of caplets in one extended palm and a glass of water in the other. I couldn't help but look at the thick outline under the towel he wrapped around his waist. *Damn, that is a serious promise under there!* He clearly told the truth, because if that monster had been inside me last night, I'd still be feeling it. *Why didn't he put on his pants or something?*

As if he heard my thoughts, he reached for his jeans and slipped them on. "You passed out cold after coming the second time. I think you needed the release pretty bad."

Sitting up, I tore open the tiny envelope and swallowed the pills, trying not to choke as I handed the water back to him. "Thank you... um... I'm not sure... ah... I don't remember very much." Shock number four: I was tongue-tied. Me. The woman who prided herself on going toe-to-toe with anyone and everyone.

He took the glass from me and put it on the nightstand. "What do you remember?"

"I had an epic fight and breakup with my boyfriend in the kitchen."

Huh, that was the understatement of the year. The truth was, we'd been fighting for months, ever since the Omni Resort Hotel hired him to be the head chef and I ended up being the sous chef. Both of us interviewed for the head job, but he landed it and became my boss.

This did not help our relationship, as I wasn't the type to play second fiddle. Especially to someone I knew for certain I could out-cook on a bad day.

My scrambling thoughts ordered themselves in somewhat of a timeline fashion. "Last night's service was a disaster. Gordon Ramsay would have had a field day. The walk-in stays a disorganized mess, and it was totally off count. A lot of food gets wasted or goes bad. I told Chase the oysters and mussels didn't smell right, but he insisted he was going to serve them anyway. I told him he shouldn't, and he started yelling at me, throwing his authority around. I yelled back, and he told me to get out of his kitchen."

The man's blue eyes grew contemplative. "I heard some people got sick in the dining room, puking their guts out. One guy had to be taken to the hospital."

Part of me felt vindicated that I was right. The other part worried about those people. Bad shellfish was some of the worst food poisoning out there.

He sat on the bed next to me, and my belly sizzled. He said we didn't have sex, yet I was intrigued by the thought. One large hand came up and ran through his hair. "You remember anything else?"

I stared at the perfect waves that settled around his face. Jeez, he looked like a cover model for one of those romance novels my friend Anita read all the time. I ignored his hotness and scrunched my face at my fuzzy recollections. "I came to the bar and told Macie what happened. He gave me a couple of shots on the house. I'm not sure after that." My face flushed. "I don't drink much, and I was on the clock, so I hadn't eaten anything substantial. I guess the liquor went to my head."

"That and something else was on your mind."

My eyes got wide. "Oh shit, what did I do? I went nuts, didn't I?"

"Sort of. You were plastered and falling down yelling about how you hadn't had a decent fuck in months and—"

"Argh!" I put my hand over his mouth to stop the flow of words. "I didn't say that out loud. Please tell me I didn't."

His pretty blue eyes looked into mine, and he nodded. "You weren't quiet about it. Pretty much everyone in the bar heard you and watched the show."

His words came out muffled behind my palm, but I knew he spoke the truth. I closed my eyes and flopped back on the bed, regretting it once my head hit the pillow.

"A couple of men were ready to help you out with that. I got you out of there before they took you up on your offer."

I groaned and covered my face with one hand while pointing at my crotch with the other. "Thank you. Um… did I do *that*?"

"No, I did. You were determined to make it happen, and I was afraid you would cut yourself. You weren't steady enough to handle a razor."

The skin between my legs itched as I recalled the

event. *"Do it. Shave it all off. I'm positive. If you don't, I'll do it myself."*

Fisting the pillow, I jammed it around my head. I had no clue what weird-ass demon possessed my brain to give me that idea. I'd been so off-kilter last night that I'd been another person entirely. "I made you do *it*, didn't I?"

I heard his chuckle through the thick foam.

"You were very demanding. You said if I didn't, you'd go back to the bar and find someone who would. Them other two could have still been down there, so I figured I was the better choice."

"Yes, oh yes. More. Do it again. Oh shit, I'm coming!" My clit twitched at the memory of his skilled tongue, and I wondered what it would be like now—this time with me completely sober.

My face flamed under the cocoon of crisp white linen. "Oh my God, I'm so sorry."

"Hey, sweetness, look at me. You're what? Five foot five, 'bout 120 pounds? Do you really think you can make me do something I don't want to do?"

I took the pillow from my face and looked at him. He was a handsome man, classic all-American football star with high cheekbones and full lips. Lips that had been on the most intimate part of my body. His eyebrow rose as if he knew where my thoughts had gone.

"I don't do this. I'm not a slut. I don't sleep around with strangers." Words poured from my mouth as a myriad of emotions hit me, embarrassment being the most predominant one. "I'm not into fucking random men I meet in bars. One-nighters. Dammit, I can't believe I let you do that much."

"Hey, darlin', slow down. Yeah, I went down on you, but I didn't do anything else. It sounds to me like you had a shitty night and needed a break. I do not mind at all, and given the circumstances, I was your safest route."

I thought about it for a moment. He was right. There were worse things than waking up to a handsome man first thing in the morning. Much worse. And in fact, I'd had a bad night after a really bad week.

Truthfully, it was more like a bunch of bad months. Eight of them. Chase had made work a nightmare. Even worse, we lived together, so we brought the tension home with us every night. The other people working in the massive kitchen of the Omni Hotel in Asheville, North Carolina, recognized I was the better person for the job, but I had two major strikes against me. Number one, I'm a woman. Number two, I'm mixed—my father's White, and my mother's Black. I'm a blend of the two, but I favored my mom's DNA more.

My word vomit continued. "What time is it? I need to go. I shouldn't be here. I'm… I'm… I'm…."

Shit, I'm going to cry.

Shock number five: I didn't cry. Ever.

Tears welled up in my eyes, and my nose promptly ran. I didn't like to lose control. Chase had accused me many times of being a control freak, but I always considered myself as being driven.

Two arms enfolded me, comforter and all. "Hey, Fauna, it's okay. No harm, no foul. You don't have to rush off. Let's take advantage of all the fancy hotel shit they got in here. We'll grab a shower and order room service. Then I'll take you where you want to go. Deal?"

His warmth seeped into my body, and I relaxed. I didn't have a job here anymore, so no schedule to keep, and no boyfriend to rush home to. This man was being incredibly kind and patient with me, so why not? I sniffed and nodded against his bare chest. *God, he smells good! How does someone do that first thing in the morning?*

"Cool. You get the shower first, and I'll order some food."

He kissed my forehead and moved to let me get up. It mildly disappointed me that he didn't kiss my lips, because I wanted to see how that felt. Probably best he didn't, as I also had the morning breath of a dead goat.

I cleared my throat as I viewed that elaborate back tattoo again. "Hey… uh… this is really, really embarrassing, but… well… you know my name, but I don't… um…"

He turned and smiled as he picked up the phone receiver. "Call me Dodge."

CHAPTER 2

Dodge ordered fluffy blueberry Belgian waffles with syrup and fruit while I showered. The morning chef was a good cook, but my stomach was rebelling enough that I didn't dare eat much. Even the rich coffee made me want to heave.

Fuck me, I'm never drinking again.

After we ate, I added another item to my list of most embarrassing moments. I didn't have any other clothes but the ones I wore to work last night: my chef's uniform. I'd left the matching flat black hat in the kitchen and probably wouldn't get it back. My black chef's pants and white custom coat stared at me from where they neatly lay across the chair along with my underwear and the sports bra I always wore underneath.

Dodge had to have been the one to lay my clothes

out so orderly. I was meticulous about order in my kitchen, but for my house, not so much. Dusting and vacuuming weren't high on my priority list, and clothes rarely made it from the laundry basket to the closet.

My nose wrinkled at the thought of putting on yesterday's panties: one of my favorite pairs, dark blue lace with a little rose accent in front. Even so, I'd worn them all day. Yuck, but it was either that or go commando like Dodge apparently did.

Suck it up, Fauna. You did it to yourself, dumbass.

The second item of the morning adding to my embarrassment list came when Dodge led me outside through the front lobby to his vehicle. The walk of shame through the ornate hotel was bad enough in my uniform and the finger-combed rat's nest on my head, but I stopped dead in my tracks when I saw what he drove. He didn't have a car—he had a motorcycle. A fucking *motorcycle*! I'd never been on one and, for the twenty-five years of my life, had never wanted to be on one. Now I didn't have a choice if I wanted a free ride home. Ubers were available, I suppose, but that cost money, and I didn't remember where I left my wallet. I had my cell phone, at least. Too bad the battery was dead.

Dodge noticed my less-than-thrilled face when he mounted the huge machine. I had to admit, it was pretty. The custom paint job showed a starry dark blue sky fading into a blazing sun resembling a chariot pulled by four flaming dragons. An intricately detailed skeleton holding a fiery sword above his head drove the chariot. Someone had put a lot of time and thought into this work. Still, the thought of getting on that bike wasn't on my bucket list of favorites.

"It's all I have here, sweetness. My other rides are at the car show today. Best I can do unless you want me to call you a cab or something."

He handed me a helmet that looked like it would swallow my head whole. The thing weighed a ton when he popped it on. His fingers traced over my throat, and he placed his hand around my larynx, finger on one side and thumb on the other. My pulse jumped at the gesture. *Fuck me, am I about to become some serial killer's next victim?* Gentle pressure had me lifting my chin, and he tightened the strap underneath.

"You have someone you want to call to come get you, or do you feel safe enough with me to get on my bike? I'll be glad to get you that rideshare if you want it."

How did he know what was in my head? "I think I'm good. I've just never ridden a motorcycle before."

His deep blue eyes bored into mine, and the

intensity in their depths would not allow me to break away. I had the privilege of having a gorgeous green-gold for an eye color, and more than one man had asked if they were real or colored contacts. "I understand if you don't trust me, Fauna, but if I was going to hurt you, I had plenty of opportunities to do that last night."

He tapped a dragon symbol on the vest he wore. The same one sat on the back. "You see this patch? This means I'm a member of the Dragon Runners Motorcycle Club. We have a strong brotherhood tighter than any blood family and an unbreakable code of ethics. Any man who earns the right to wear this cut is one you can trust with your life."

He said this with enough conviction and sincerity that I relaxed. No, I wasn't about to become a media headline on the daily newsfeed. In reality, he was right in that he'd had plenty of time to hurt me when I was blackout wasted last night.

He strapped on a much smaller helmet and patted the tiny pad behind him for me to sit.

Shit, can I be more awkward trying to get on a bike for the first time in my life with what seems like twenty extra pounds on my head?

I somehow settled myself behind him and put my feet where he pointed. The next challenge was where to put my hands. I placed them on his shoulders, and he immediately pulled them down to wrap tightly around his waist. This pulled my crotch up against his butt, and I gasped from the hot contact.

I had no time to reposition and try to get a sliver of space between us before he fired up the engine and took off with a roar of pipes. A "Holy shit" erupted out of my mouth as I slid backward and clutched him hard. I could have sworn he laughed at me.

It was early summer, and the temperatures were rising. The day was turning out to be beautiful. A sunny, clear sky hung overhead. Green leafy trees decorated the blue with texture, and contrasting colors of pink, white, and red wildflowers that grew in the highway median flashed as we zoomed by. The man between my legs steered the rumbling behemoth under us with precision and care. I watched his hands move when he switched gears. When he leaned into a curve, I leaned with him, following his movements. I became super aware of his body, his hard stomach under my fingers, the flex of his muscles, and my breasts pressed firmly against his back. My pussy itched, probably from its recent shaving, and I had to fight the urge to grind it against his butt for relief. Dodge's uncanny perception of me kicked in, and he placed a hand over mine for a hot minute as if to say *"Hang on, sweetness, we're almost there."*

His GPS led us right to the condo where Chase and I lived. My old Honda sat in my spot, and I didn't see Chase's brand-new Audi anywhere. I breathed a sigh of relief. Another confrontation was on the horizon, but I didn't want to face it any sooner than necessary.

Guilt ate at me from my behavior last night, and my stomach rolled as reality set in. Chase had fired me and told me to get the hell out of his kitchen and his condo.

"Who the fuck do you think you are questioning me?" *The metal spatula rang when he threw it against the far wall.*

I didn't flinch at the noise, but my next statement came from between gritted teeth. "I don't have to question anything. The seafood is bad. Smell it."

"It's dated for tomorrow."

"Well, someone got it wrong. You serve that, you'll make people sick."

"The only person wrong is you. I'm sick of your attitude. I'm the fuckin' boss, and you need to learn to respect that."

Liquid sloshed from the bowl as I slammed it down. "You want respect? How 'bout earning it? The refrigerator is filthy with spoiled food. You cook from frozen instead of fresh in a city that's considered a foodie mecca. The kitchen hasn't had a good cleaning in weeks, and the menu is too fuckin' big to be any good. How the hell did you ever get to be a chef?"

Chase's face turned scarlet red, like an overripe tomato. "You goddamn bitch, get the fuck out! You're fired. Get your shit outta my house by Monday or else I'm burning it all."

"You don't need to fire me, asshole. I quit. I'm done with you, your shitty-ass food, and your fucking cocky attitude. Everyone knows I'm the better chef."

"You okay, sweetness?"

Dodge's words cut through the memory and brought me to the present where I stood.

I shook off my reverie and handed him his helmet. "Yes, I'm fine."

"You don't look fine, baby. You look like you want to run or hurl."

I laughed despite my churning gut and aching head. "I'm good, Dodge. Thanks for all you did last night… um… I mean, keeping me from doing something worse. Not… ah…" *Well, really, that too.*

He grinned, and my breath caught. *Damn, he is a fine-looking man!*

"No problem with any of it, sweetness. You have your keys to get in?"

"The door has a keypad."

He grunted and shifted on the bike. "I'm not cool 'bout leavin' you here by yourself. You sure you're okay?"

Handsome, built like a brick shithouse, and super nice. *Oh God, why didn't I meet this man before Chase?*

I put on my game face. "Truly, I'm fine. You go do your thing. I'm gonna do mine."

"Fauna."

He stared into my face in silence for a minute. I could tell from his expression that he truly didn't like the idea of riding away. His attention and his obvious need to protect flattered me. But I was still a grown-ass woman, and the demons I had to face belonged to me and me alone. "Dodge, I'm good. I promise."

"I'm leaving this afternoon to go back home. All my business cards are at the car show. You want my number in case you need help or somethin'? I can write it down."

Fuck me, he was so fine and seemed to be such a good man, but I'd already made some terrible choices and didn't need anymore. I shook my head. "The last forty-eight hours have been rather rough. I have a lot to think about and some decisions to make. Let's just consider this to be a fond memory of the one who got away, yeah?"

His lips pressed together. "If that's what you

want, sweetness. Have a nice life, and good luck with everything."

He raised his helmet to put it on, and I stopped him. "Dodge? Thank you for saving my ass and being such a great guy. That means more to me than I can ever say."

I leaned in and placed my mouth on his, intending on a simple goodbye kiss. He slid a gloved hand behind my head and sweetly took over. His tongue teased against my lips, and I didn't resist opening for him. Some women described kissing as lightning strikes, sparks, zings, and other flashes. Dodge's kiss was none of these. His was a long, slow broil that started in my stomach and spread through my body. I bet he made love the same way. Too bad this was all I'd ever get. Even the memory of his mouth between my legs held a promise I couldn't keep.

The kiss ended, and I backed away, covering my shakiness with a smile and a flippant wave. "Take care and be safe."

He stayed silent while he put on his helmet. Nope, he still didn't want to go. I bet he would stay in a heartbeat with only one word from me. I kept quiet.

He pulled away from the curb, and with a flick of his fingers, he drove off. The sound from his motorcycle faded, and I moved to punch in the condo's code. My squishy middle held all the feels ever made. Sadness. Regret. Hope. Desire. All of them blended into one big confusing ball. Bleh, I needed to get my head on straight. I had work to do and a life to get on track.

I expected the condo to be empty when I entered, but an unmistakable noise greeted me. Three large garbage bags sat by the front door with all my clothes spilling out from the top. Chase was home after all and had been busy.

Hmph. I thought he said I had until Monday. Fucker must have changed his mind. Asshole.

My turbo charger sat in the small kitchen, and I climbed the steps to get there and plug in my phone. The condo had this weird modern design where each room stacked up in a column: utility and foyer on the bottom, kitchen and living areas next, then the main bedroom, and a final small extra area on top that opened to the roof. A tight spiral staircase joined them, and I never liked the sense of being closed in. I guess now I didn't have to deal with it.

While I was in the kitchen, I pulled out my spare set of keys, packed my spare knives and a few other personal cooking implements, and added them to the pile at the door. It took me about ten minutes tops to get the bags and other stuff loaded in my car. I'd go through the haphazard pile later, but there was one item I'd noticed was missing, and there was no way I was leaving without it.

The noise was still going strong upstairs, and I straightened my shoulders to brave it out. My leaden feet made the trip up to the next level. I turned the corner and got a full view of the loud source. Chase's pale behind was pumping frantically into one of the servers. She was young, strawberry blonde, pretty, and had been flirting with Chase for months. I suspected this was not the first time they were together based on their behavior at work.

She lay under him and put on a real show. Her head thrashed from side to side, and she moaned, cried out, whimpered, and gasped better than any porn star on film. Me? I was surprisingly unhurt. I just didn't care. Maybe I never really did. I had no moral leg to stand on anyway, as just hours after Chase and I broke up, I was in a bed with a total stranger.

Neither of them noticed as I crept to the dresser and pulled down the antique jewelry box my grandmother gave me before she died. I opened the top and saw it was still full. Chase had probably overlooked it in his haste to get me out. I moved close enough to see the girl suddenly bow up and scream.

She scrunched up her face, whipped her head harder, clawing at Chase's arms.

"*Oh!* Oh, oh, oh, yes! Oh yes! Give it to me, baby! Oh yes!"

Seriously? I rolled my eyes hard enough to hurt. "He's not all that, girlfriend. Better get yours first, 'cause I can guarantee he's a one-and-done kinda man. He'll take all the blow jobs you want to give, but you'll be waiting a long time for him to go down on you."

Chase stopped his frantic thrusting and jerked at the comforter to cover his ass. "Goddammit, Fauna!"

"Oh my gawd! She was watchin' us!"

The shouts and squeals of outrage were music to my ears, and I laughed, twiddling my fingers in a wave as I left the scrambling couple. I grabbed my half-charged phone and charger on the way out. Chase called something down the stairs, but I didn't hear it as I marched out the door.

A minute later, I climbed in my car and drove away. Numbness settled in, and for a few moments I was okay, but then my gut roiled, and I had to pull over at the complex entrance. I had just enough time to get the door open before my stomach emptied itself on the median grass.

Fuck me, I hate vomiting!

I waited to make sure round two wasn't coming up, then powered up my phone.

"Hola, chica. Whatchoo doin' calling me on a workday?" Anita's voice was a balm to my ears.

"Bad time, girlfriend. I need a place to stay for a few days."

"*Chingada.* You finally got your head outta your ass and broke up with the *pendejo*?"

"Epically."

Anita puffed out a sigh. "Madre de Dios, it's about time. Connie keeps a spare key under the ugly garden statue at the house. I'll text her now and let her know you'll be staying with us for a while. Is it a beer night or tequila?"

The thought of more alcohol made my head throb, but the occasion still called for some liquid courage. "Beer. I had enough liquor last night to last me a long time."

"That bad?"

"Worse, but I'll tell you later."

"I want all the details. I have three more jobs today, but I'll get home as soon as I can. Adios, mi amiga. We'll get you straight."

She hung up, and I tapped my phone screen to close the app.

Details?

A picture of Dodge's face appeared in my brain,

and I sifted through the recollections of the previous night. Dodge's hands on my body, his mouth on my breasts, his tongue between my legs.

Nope. I would tell Connie and Anita about the breakup and this morning, but I wanted to keep my biker as a private memory.

Wait, my *biker?*

Meh, I guess I could privately call him that since I would never see him again.

CHAPTER 3

The chitter of nighttime katydids filled the air as Dodge opened the door to his apartment and tossed his keys on the table. The complex was old but affordable, and he didn't need much. The main living space had an open floor plan that included the kitchen and living and dining areas all in one big room. The small space looked bigger from the lack of furniture and no clutter, just a plain kitchen table with two chairs, a sofa, and a big flat-screen TV and entertainment center. His bedroom held a queen-size bed, a nightstand, and a chest of drawers. The few pictures and posters on the walls were of vintage motorcycles and muscle cars.

He opened the refrigerator door to look at the contents. Nope, it hadn't changed since he left for the car show. A half loaf of bread of questionable age, an unwrapped block of dried out cheese, packets of different take-out condiments, and two six-packs of his favorite beer. He grabbed a dark brown bottle and let the door shut. The cap twisted off easily, and he snapped it between two fingers, sending it across the room into the open trash can.

Fuck, he was tired. Car shows were a fun time and generated a lot of business for the MC's custom shop, but they took a lot out of him.

He shuffled through the delivery menus to see who was still open at this time of night. Not many other than pizza joints. He opened the app on his phone and made his order. Pizza wasn't his first choice, but it was cheap, filling, and available.

His mouth opened in a giant cow yawn as he settled on the sofa and clicked on the TV. Shit, only twenty-eight years old and he was ready to call it a night. He used to go hard until the early morning hours and then still work a full day. Not so much now.

While he waited for his food, he pulled out his phone and scrolled through the pictures of the cars at the show. Two of his custom paint jobs had placed in the competition, and he'd found some parts he needed for a '67 Mustang he had in the shop. He'd also picked up a '59 Karmen Ghia that someone abandoned in a field to rot. The top had been left open and the interior was ruined, but all the parts were there, and the engine was original. He'd bought it for a song and would spend at least a year on its restoration. In the end, he would make a sweet profit on the classic car.

His thumb moved through the photos until one popped up, and he paused. It was a pic of Fauna he had taken on impulse last night. She had fallen dead asleep after coming hard for the second time and lay in a tangle of sheets that only covered her hips, her hair spread out around her head and her lips slightly parted. Dark nipples topped her small breasts. He recalled her breathy gasps as she clutched at his head between her legs. It had been a very long time since he'd last touched a woman with any kind of intimacy, and he was happy to know he still had his skills.

She looked peaceful in the picture. Beautiful.

When she first stomped into the bar in her chef uniform, Dodge noticed her. Gorgeous with her head held high as a queen and ready for a fight. Her radiant coffee skin drew his attention like a lodestone. She'd torn a black hat off a head full of tight, springy curls and threw it on the bar, her deep gold-and-green eyes snapping. By her body language and expression, she was not in a good mood. He sat close enough to hear her sharp complaints to the bartender.

"Fucker just fired me. I swear, Macie, one of these days he's going to kill someone with the nasty shit he calls food."

"I been tellin' you to drop his ass for months, girlfriend." He poured her a shot of tequila and set a saltshaker next to it. He shouted over his shoulder as he moved to the other end of the bar to scoop up a few lemon wedges on a napkin, "I hope this little drama means what I think it means."

Dodge watched as the woman licked the back of her hand and sprinkled salt on it. "Yep, it abso-fuckin-lutely does. I. Am. Done." She threw back the shot and gasped. "Holy shit. I forgot how strong you pour, but I want another." Her white teeth bit into a lemon wedge as the bartender gave her a refill.

Dodge recalled there'd been two other men at the bar who took note of her quick consumption as well. He'd intended to finish his own drink and go to his hotel room by himself, but the woman started spouting all sorts of shit to the bartender. They seemed to be friends, as she didn't hold back at all: the kitchen, the bad food, the fight, the lack of intimacy in her life, her struggles as a woman of color, and on and on. Her slurred words and loss of control escalated quickly. Too quickly, Dodge decided. She was on the small side and maybe not used to alcohol despite the classic tequila drinking method. A career drinker wouldn't get that drunk that fast on two shots of Patrón. The other men were eyeing her with a speculation Dodge recognized. The two of them stared at the woman and whispered between themselves, lust clearly on their faces. He didn't want to get involved but couldn't leave her alone to be taken advantage of by two strangers in a bar.

One man made a gesture of thrusting the index finger of one hand through a circle he made with the other. When he added a second finger, Dodge had the impulse to take the bastard outside and beat the ever-loving shit out of him. But that would have left her alone, and she was getting louder and drunker.

He was still surprised it only took two shots before she was hammered. It was a piece of cake to get her to his room, and he meant for her to pass out and sleep it off. She had other plans.

"I got people aroun' me all the time, an' I'm still lonely. Even my fuckin' boyfriend leaves me alone. He's nodda good cook. Not ad' all. Gonna make people sick. Can't run a kitchen. I got better scores in cullenurry… coolnory… fuck. Cooking school. More essperience. Only reezon he got through id is 'cauz I helped him with hiz food. I was 'posed to get the head chef job. Been working my ass off for it, but noooo! He geds it. Story of my life, I guess, and no one

cares. I work hard, keep my noze clean, an' still I'm at the bahdom. My las' boyfrien' did the same. He cheaded on me too. I'm sooo tired of bein' overlooked. Fuck it, I need to feel somethin'. I need to feel someone."

Dodge's thumb hovered over the Delete button. Fauna had begged him to fuck her, insisted on shaving herself, and threatened to go back to the bar to find someone else when he refused. Short of using physical restraining force, he had little choice if he wanted to protect her. Twice he went down on her, and twice she came hard in his mouth. Dodge licked his lips as he recalled her rich flavor. His cock had swelled to painful hardness, and he'd slipped into the bathroom, fisted himself, and quickly found his own release.

He took the picture on his phone after he came back in the bedroom and saw her sleeping. Yeah, it was creeper-ish, but he didn't think about that at the time.

This morning, she was contrite and embarrassed. He thought about just making her leave, but there was something vulnerable about her. Some need she had, and he found himself in rescue mode, feeding her breakfast and then taking her home. She didn't cling or want his number, which surprised him. Definitely not what he was used to, and he'd been kinda disappointed.

He'd thought about her words during the final hours of the car show as he packed up to head home.

"Let's just consider this to be a fond memory of the one who got away, yeah?"

He hoped it was that simple, but it didn't seem to be going that way if she was still on his mind.

"Thank you for saving my ass and being such a great guy. That means more to me than I can ever say."

Three knocks sounded on the door and disturbed his musings. Dodge got up, thinking it was the pizza he ordered. He opened the door and wished he'd looked through the peephole first. Blood rushed to his head, and his hand clenched the doorknob. He wanted to both slam it shut and open it wide at the same time. What were the odds that the minute he might have found something new and bright, something old showed up?

"Hey, baby. Gonna let me in?"

"What are you doing here, Mallory?"

The woman's lower lip pushed out, making a red duck mouth. "I haven't seen you in a while. Thought I'd come by for a spell."

Dodge's jaw tightened as he saw the dilation of her blue eyes. "It's awfully late for a friendly visit. How long you been in town?"

Mallory ignored his question and pushed her way into the apartment. "Bedelia said you was at some car thing all weekend, an' I figured you was back by now. Get anything good?"

"Some."

"Hmmm, that's cool. You've always been real smart about bikes and cars and stuff."

She flopped down on the sofa and slipped off her high wedge shoes. Dodge watched with his hand still on the open door as she dropped a worn leather jacket on the floor and settled in. She appeared skinnier than the last time he'd seen her. Even her breasts seemed smaller from the way her shadowy nipples poked out under her tight Harley tank top. The short, ripped jean skirt she wore rucked up and showed her see-through black leggings. She wasn't wearing full panties but a thong.

"Hey, baby? You got any food?"

He wasn't surprised at her hunger. This wasn't the first time she'd come to him this way. "Ordered a pizza. Should be here soon."

"Cool. You got any beer?"

A tickle of dread brushed the back of his neck. If the universe wanted to fuck with him, it had picked a great time. "I'll ask again, Mallie. What are you doin' here?"

She looked up at him, and her lips quivered. "Been living up in Iron Duff for a while now. It's not too far away, so I thought I'd come home for a bit. I was hopin' you'd let me stay here for a little while."

"This hasn't been your home in a long time."

Tears dripped down her cheek, leaving dark streaks behind. "The truth is the guy I was stayin' with kicked me out. Had to sleep in my car 'cause I ain't got no place to go 'cept here. I ain't got no money either. I'm hopin' you'll take me in at least until I get on my feet."

Dodge closed his eyes and took a deep breath through his nose. How many years had he repeated this same cycle? She'd been in and out of his life since childhood, only coming back to him when she had no other options. At one time, he thought they would be together forever, and she was the love of his life. That dream shattered almost from the beginning, and he'd spent many nights picking up the pieces. Too many. His head told him to not care and tell her to leave, but his damn heart wouldn't listen.

"Hey, bro. Got your pizza." The delivery driver showed up in the open doorway. The college student's eyes got big at the sight of Mallory lounging on the sofa, but he kept his comments to himself. The kid had talked to Dodge more than once about prospecting with the Dragon Runners and had learned the art of discretion.

Dodge pulled his wallet out of his back pocket

and pulled out two twenties. The tip was more than the pizza price, but Dodge knew the young man was working two jobs to make ends meet while still going to school. "Thanks, kid. Be safe out there."

The driver nodded once, and with a last look at Mallory, he left.

Dodge waved Mallory over and put the box on the middle cushion.

"You need a coffee table, baby."

I need a lot of things. Balls would be a good start.

He reached for the roll of paper towels he kept by the sofa and tore off several. "You worked anywhere lately?"

Mallory frowned. "I had a job at a Quickmart back in Iron Duff for a while. Got fired 'cause I was late a few times. I ain't been lookin' for 'nother one yet, but I'll get on that tomorrow. Promise."

Dodge tore off a bite of pizza. He'd experienced firsthand how much her promises were worth. It wasn't in him to kick her out, though. The thought of her living on the streets or in her car bothered him too much. The protector in him rose to the top. "You can stay here for a few days until you find a job. That's it, Mallie. Take the bedroom, and I'll take the couch."

She gave him a side-eye that he guessed was supposed to be sexy as she lifted a slice of pizza.

"You don't gotta sleep out here, baby. I'm happy to share." Her tongue darted out to touch the tip of the triangle and deliberately circled it before she bit into the crust.

Dodge recognized the tactic she used over and over again to get what she wanted, from him or some other sucker who got caught up in her web. He forced down the lump of food in his throat and took another bite. He knew what she was and yet he still let her come back, time after time. She was his first love, his longest hurt, and his biggest weakness.

She finished two big slices and stretched, the thin tank going transparent as she arched her back and thrust out her chest. "Mmm… I'm so tired."

Here it comes.

Dodge held another slice of pizza as she stood up and whipped the tank over her head. A pink jewel winked at him where it dangled from her left nipple. That was new. She traced her fingers over her shoulders and down to the piercing, flicking it lightly. "Wanna come tuck me in?"

He hated it. Hated that she had this power over him. Hated being so weak when it came to her. Hated the games she played and how he fell for them again and again. Most of all, he hated himself for still caring about her.

Not this time. I swear, no more.

"I'm staying out here. You go on to bed."

She pouted again. "Sure you don't want me to pay for my dinner?"

The bite he took threatened to rise. How many times had she "paid" for stuff this way with other men? "No, Mallie. I'm done, and I have to work tomorrow."

Her face bowed up like she wanted to say something else. Then she let it go and shrugged. "Suit yourself. The invite is there if you want it."

She peeled off the leggings, leaving her completely naked save for the tiny black strings crossing over her skinny hips. He watched her saunter into his bedroom, the twin flat planes of her ass moving as she did. His dick twitched with some interest at the sight of a bare and willing female, even though he wasn't into stick-figure women. Dodge gritted his teeth in anger as his body betrayed him. The last thing he needed was to get involved with Mallie again, but it was second nature to him to take care of her.

With a soft curse, he lifted himself off the sofa to straighten up his apartment and ignore the woman in his bedroom. He put away the leftover pizza and crushed the box into the trash can. Mallory had left the two articles of clothing on the floor. He picked them up, folded them neatly, and placed them on the kitchen counter. Jesus, how many times had he done this? Picked up after her for years, and not just clothes?

He had to walk through his bedroom to get to the bathroom. She smiled at him as she slipped under the covers. The bristles on his toothbrush were wet, and he guessed Mallory had helped herself. He kept a pack of extras under the sink and pulled out a new one. The cap was already off on the toothpaste tube, and he found it on the floor next to the discarded hand towel. He replaced the cap and hung the towel back up.

Only a few days. I swear, only a few days.

She was in his queen-size bed and had artfully arranged the sheets to bare her upper half. "Last chance, honey. Sure you don't want to share?"

He reached for a pillow and snagged the folded quilt he kept at the end of the bed. "I'm sure."

Back in the main room, he stripped completely. He always slept naked and preferred to go commando during the day. The sofa didn't fit his large frame, and he struggled to find a comfortable position.

His head berated him over and over about letting Mallory into the small apartment. He supposed he could leave her there and go to the Lair for the night. The Lair was the Dragon Runners' compound and clubhouse. As a full patched member, he had a room for his personal use and stayed there whenever he wanted. But it was late, his eyes were gritted with fatigue, and he didn't want to ride that far. Plus, he didn't trust Mallory not to snoop through his stuff and take something. She had before.

He punched the pillow and shifted on his back to stare at the ceiling. *Fuck, why did I let her in?* The plain white sheetrock had no answers. He finally fell into a fitful sleep.

HE WOKE UP IN THE DARK TO A MOUTH WRAPPED around his hard cock, sucking him deep. Teeth, tongue, and lips all worked together, seeking the most sensitive part of his head. A hand cupped and expertly massaged his balls. He barely made out the woman's head bobbing over his middle. A flash of Fauna's beautiful face appeared in his half-awake brain, and he groaned out loud at the pleasure building between his legs. His cock swelled larger as he got closer and closer to climax. Fuck, it felt so damn good, and it had been so long! His balls tightened and his lower spine sparked in brief warning that he was about to blow.

He reached a hand to the head working him. "I'm coming, sweet—"

Dry straw crisped under his fingers, not the springy soft curls he was expecting.

His mind was fully awake now. Mallory. Not Fauna.

But he was too far gone to stop. She took him to the back of her throat, and he let loose, shooting hard, crying out in pleasure and frustration. She swallowed everything he gave her, sucking him dry. He was wrung out limp when she finally released him.

He stayed silent. She draped herself across him, snuggling in, and his arms automatically closed around her. "Love you, baby. It's so good to be home." Her sleepy voice faded. "I'm gonna make it right this time. Promise."

Dodge lay there under her lax body, her small breasts pressing into his chest. He was uncomfortable as hell, but if he moved, he would end up dumping her on the floor. Some men might do that. He couldn't.

He stretched out his arm and snagged his phone. With Mallory lightly snoring, face down on top of him, he scrolled through his pictures until he got to the one of Fauna.

For several seconds he stared at it, his head full of regret.

"Let's just consider this to be a fond memory of the one that got away, yeah?"

He closed his eyes, his mind filled with wishes that would never come true. He sensed a familiar tightening in his chest as if chains locked around him.

Then he pressed Delete.

CHAPTER 4

"I HAVE AN IDEA FOR YOU. WHAT DO YOU THINK ABOUT owning your own place?" Anita sprayed and wiped off the dresser. She tossed her cleaning rag into the plastic bag to join the others. The door was open to the bathroom where I was working, and we conversed as we cleaned.

I tapped the brush on the edge of the toilet and flushed. "Not much. Why?"

"You met my sister, Connie, right? She and her boyfriend were talking the other night about some restaurant for sale he used to go to over in Bryson City. Some old woman owned it, but she's in a nursing home, and none of the kids are interested in keeping it. Apparently, it's been all but abandoned, and the family just wants it sold. Sounds to me like they'd take whatever offer they got to be rid of it."

I dumped blue powder into the sink and started scouring the built-up toothpaste globs at the bottom. "What is it? Some little greasy spoon that serves burgers and hot dogs to tourists?"

Anita plugged in the vacuum. "Does it matter? If it's your place, you can do whatever you want, right?"

I turned on the faucet and watched the mess gurgle away down the drain as Anita moved into the bedroom with the heavy machine.

"Think about it, chica. What else you got going here? That *pendejo* you were living with has spread it around the city that you're trouble. You've applied everywhere, and no one is calling you back. Even if someone hired you, I think you'd still be in the same spot—a secondary chef no one will take seriously." Her ponytail whipped back and forth as she sighed and shook her head. "As far as women have come this century, there are still some places that judge you by what's between your legs instead of what's in your brain."

She fired up the machine, and the noise negated any more conversation. Anita and her sister, Connie Martinez, were two Mexican American women who had their own housecleaning business. I'd met them at the Omni when they were hired as independent contractors once when the hotel had a worker shortage. Anita's constant sunny outlook and positive energy drew everyone in around her, and she gave me a lot of support as Chase and I went through our rough patches. After the contract ended, we stayed in touch, becoming fast friends. When I left the condo with all my stuff, Anita was the first person I called. Her immediate response was to let me stay with her and Connie. Connie spent most of her free time with the boyfriend I'd never met, so I stayed in her room for now.

They were great house cleaners with a solid reputation. They had a small army of workers to take care of their many private clients and still had a waiting list. I helped since I'd been staying with Anita rent free for the past few weeks, but this was not my calling. Eventually, I would have to make a decision and move on.

I wiped off the granite countertop as thoughts crowded my mind. *Own my own restaurant? Running an established kitchen as a chef is a lot of work. Turning one around is even more. Building one from scratch? I can only imagine it would own my life. Front of house, servers, sous chefs, maybe a bartender, and then there's the menu, purchasing the supplies, equipment, decor, ingredients —it's endless.* "What's the name of the place? Do you know?"

Anita grinned and yelled over the vacuum's noise, "No, but it can't be that hard to find."

We did four houses, and by the time we got back to Anita and Connie's place, I was ready for a shower and bed. They tried to talk me into going out to a bar for drinks and dancing, but I waved them off. Those two had more energy than I could keep up with. I wasn't in bad shape, and perhaps I might have mustered up the stamina, but I needed some alone time to think.

It's funny how cleaning houses all day made me feel dirty. After my shower, I put on my favorite panties and an old tank top and settled on Connie's queen-size bed. I opened my laptop and googled restaurants for sale in Bryson City. A listing and picture for The Diner popped up. That was it. The Diner. No website or menu. Yelp had a generic listing for it, stating it was indeed a burger, sandwich, and hot dog kind of place. The three reviews were old and lukewarm but not disparaging. I figured that was both a plus and a minus. Not enough customers to leave bad remarks for a poor rating, but the point was just that—not enough customers.

I examined the few pictures online and google-mapped the place to get a satellite view. Red brick facade, large square planters out front with dead plants, worn-out canopies over the large front windows, and a few plastic patio tables and chairs on the wide sidewalk. There was nothing impressive about the look of it. If the inside was as bad as the outside, it would have to go through a major renovation.

The word *bistro* popped into my head. Upscale casual. I pictured the front all cleaned up with rounded tables and ornate chairs to match, umbrellas and tablecloths in forest green to contrast with the red brick. French cuisine was my forte, but I knew local ingredients were always a good marketable item and usually the freshest and most available. I leaned back in the bed, musing. Cornmeal-crusted rainbow mountain trout, served on a bed of red garlic quinoa and fennel salad. Simple but filling. Coq au vin with sautéed haricot vert and pearl onions. A thick hearty beef bourguignon served with fresh salad and warm yeasty baguette. Classic croque monsieur sandwich and onion soup. Local wines paired with each dish, and a good selection of craft beers. Crepes with cherry or Nutella filling—

My phone's ring cut through my fantasy restaurant planning. I glanced at the Hello Kitty clock on the wall: 10:00 p.m. Shit, only one of two people would dare to call me at this hour. I looked at the number to confirm before I answered. "Hello, Mother."

"I heard they fired you."

Yup, a classic Harriet Somers greeting. No "Hi" or "How are you?" or "Are you okay?" with her. Straight to the point, do not pass Go or collect two hundred dollars.

"Yes, they did. About three weeks ago. Chase and I had a fight at work, and he canned me."

"What did you do?"

My hand tightened on my phone, and my face burned. This was also typical of my mother. If something went wrong in my life, no matter what the circumstance, it had to be my fault. "I did my job, Mother. Nothing more than that."

Thankfully she dropped it, at least for now. My mother kept a cache of all slights, wrongdoings, arguments, and past conversations to use as weapons in the future. Tonight she pulled out her favorite one.

"To this day, I cannot understand why you chose to be a chef. You could have been a doctor like your brother. Such a waste of talent."

The burn in my face increased. "Mother, we've been over this. I didn't want to be a doctor. I love what I do, and I'm good at it."

She huffed. "Yes, you're a good cook. I'm a good cook, but I didn't have to go to culinary school to be one."

"Being a chef is more complicated than that. I—"

"Are you coming for your father's birthday celebration?"

Dismissed. Again. "I'll try."

"We will expect you on Thursday night. Where are you working now? I assume you got another position. Head chef this time?"

"Uh… no, not yet. Chase kicked me out of the condo when we broke up. I've been staying with my friends Anita and Connie." I braced myself. *Here it comes in three… two…*

"Those *maids*? Oh, Fauna, don't tell me you're cleaning houses now!"

"I've been helping with some jobs, yes. It's honest work for good pay. There's nothing wrong with that. Lots of people make a living working in services."

"Oh, for the love of God, Fauna. It's menial labor! It's bad enough for you to be working in a kitchen. You're a Somers. I hope no one we know has seen you or, God forbid, hired you."

Her exasperated tone set my teeth on edge. "I doubt that's gonna happen since you and Dad live in Charlotte."

"Your father is a top vice president of an internationally recognized bank. Hundreds of people know and respect him. I can't imagine what they would think if they knew his only daughter was a *domestic*."

She whisper-hissed *domestic* as if the syllables

would burn her mouth. At one time in my life, her scathing comments filled me with shame. My grades were never good enough. Only first place counted at my high school track meets, and I didn't win them often. My academic standing was too low. I needed to straighten and tame my curly hair more. I needed to be thinner. My clothes weren't fashionable enough. I spent my life under her microscopic scrutiny, and any perceived flaw was expressly forbidden. The only worthy professions were that of a doctor or lawyer, and her anger at me still raged on from when I went to the culinary academy and not medical school.

I was so over it. "Actually, Mom, I'm looking at a different path now."

She ignored the *Mom* dig. I used the word because I knew she hated it. *Mother* was her preferred moniker. "Oh? Have you come to your senses at last and decided to go back to medical school? I'm sure your father can pull some strings at Duke and get you in for the fall semester."

"No, I'm not cut out to be a doctor, Mom. There's a cute little diner for sale in Bryson City. I'm going to buy it."

Her silence had an ear-shattering volume. Then she spoke in her grittiest voice. "A *diner*? Are you completely out of your mind?"

I gripped my phone tighter with a little guilt, as this was my first reaction when Anita broached the idea to me.

My mom continued her tirade. "Bryson City? Never heard of it."

"It's a small town west of here in the Smoky Mountains. It's really cute. Google it sometime. I'm driving up there tomorrow and checking it out."

"How do you expect to pay for this… this… *diner*?"

"I'll get a business loan. I'm sure Dad can pull those strings just as well as he could Duke's."

"Your father and I will not cosign any loans for you to throw away on a cheap diner," she sneered.

"Then I'll use my trust fund."

"We'll never approve it."

"I don't think you can keep me from using my own money."

"Fauna, you need to stop this nonsense at once and come home before you embarrass us any further. You? Own a restaurant? A diner? Ridiculous."

There it was. I was the black sheep of the family and a failure in their eyes. My brother rarely spoke to me, and I hadn't seen my father much since I went to culinary school. Only for the token holiday here and there to make pretty family pictures for the obligatory postcards Mom always sent. None of my family came to my graduation.

"I'm sorry you feel that way, Mom. I need to go. I have a long drive tomorrow and a lot to do."

The phone went dead in my hand. No "Goodbye" or "Good luck."

I swiped the screen closed and put it on the tiny nightstand. My sinuses stung, but I didn't cry. I learned a long time ago that tears solved nothing.

The pics of the restaurant still showed on my laptop, along with the address and phone number of the realtor. I sniffed once, just because, and opened a new tab for Google Maps—this time for driving directions.

CHAPTER 5

Dodge sighed and swore under his breath as he peeled another sheet from his sketchbook, crumpled it up, and stuffed it in his pocket. The Lair was filled with the anticipation of the big summer tourist season, and the party atmosphere sat thick in the air. Mute and Bruiser were down at the River's Edge Bar while Betsey had the night off and was manning the bar here at the Lair. The queen in her kingdom. Brick held court in the main room as he shot a game of pool with Table. Stud and Hollywood were battling it out in a video game with several club women cheering them on.

Dodge spotted Donna as she sidled up to the newest and youngest member, Rafter. He'd been given his full membership patch this week. It was a bit like watching a mountain lion stalk its prey. Definitely a cougar moment.

The noise usually didn't bother him, but for some reason, tonight he was restless. Probably because he was hiding. There was plenty of work at the garage to put in overtime, but even he had to sleep at some point. The truth was he didn't want to go home. Reason number one was Mallory's presence. She was still there even after the deadline he'd given her.

Who was he kidding? Any time he'd thought about making her leave in the past, he never had the strength to do it. It just wasn't in him. It would be like kicking an eager puppy.

He threw the wadded ball into the nearest trash can and started over. The client wanted a giant multi-colored spider on the hood of his classic Pontiac. Dodge planned on graphing it later, but he wanted to give the owner a few possibilities. If he'd gone home, he doubted he would have gotten anything done.

She'd gotten a job at a local chain grocery store and so far had stayed there, but her job history was sketchy. Seldom had she kept working at anything long term. A few months at most. Once, she'd worked at a convenience store for just over a year, but that was the longest she ever stayed employed.

Another reason was her pushiness for them to become intimate. In the past, he gave in more than once during her sporadic invasions into his life. Each time, just when he thought there was a glimmer of them working out, she disappeared. His heart had been broken and healed enough times that he didn't think it would ever work again.

That was until the most recent car show over in Asheville.

He picked up a pencil and drew a few lines. Rounded abdomen, long legs, gold-green colors.

Fuck, I have to stop daydreaming.

"Heard Cathy over at the real estate office say someone called her today 'bout Mae's old diner. Sucks for anyone buying that place. Need a whole lotta work to get it goin' again," Molly announced as she gathered her purse and car keys. She was Cutter's old lady, one of the oldest and highest respected members of the club. "I gotta get to the station. Cain't wait until I get off these night shifts."

Molly worked as a part-time dispatcher at the sheriff's office. Some townspeople thought it was weird for the club to have any connections with law enforcement, but somehow, they made it work.

Dodge shaded the abdomen for deeper perception, smudged the edges of the sketch with his finger, and then started drawing an eye in the middle of the abdomen. His thoughts wandered to the last time he'd gazed into a pair of them that intrigued him enough to stay in his memory. Almond-shaped, rare and appealing color, surrounded by thick black lashes that were real instead of glued-on fakes, Fauna's image had cropped up in his mind from time to time over the last few weeks. He hated that he left her that morning, alone in front of her home. What was she doing now? Did she and her boyfriend make up, or did she find another job? She seemed to be a capable woman despite the drunk show in the bar. He was still surprised at how little alcohol it took to get her that way, but again, he put it down to her small size and not used to drinking. It would have taken a hard drinker a lot more than the two small shots she'd taken.

Yeah, the one who got away. She was probably better off since his life had gotten complicated. Again. It was hard to start a new relationship when the old one kept cropping up.

Dodge let his fingers work as he detailed the pair of eyes that took over the paper. A long nose with a small stud in the side, high cheekbones surrounded by a bunch of springy curls, full lips in an angry pout.

Nope.

He turned his pencil over and erased the down-turned mouth, then drew in a smiling one. That was more like it. This was what he wanted to keep in his memory. It would fade over time, but for now, he drew her as he wanted to see her.

A text buzzed his phone, and the moment shattered.

> Dad: Need you to come by the house tomorrow.

Dodge sighed again as his concentration was broken. He texted back.

> Dodge: I'm working until 6:00 tomorrow. What's your time frame?

> Dad: I guess it can wait until 6:30.

No explanation of whatever his dad wanted, but Dodge was positive it had to be something physical. He stood, and several vertebrae realigned themselves as he stretched. Another text came in, this one from Mallory.

> Mallory: You comin home?

Home. Was it really his anymore?

> Dodge: Already at the Lair. I'll crash here tonight.

He turned off the phone to get some peace from

the texts and walked down the hallway to his room. The bed creaked as he settled on it and tucked the two big pillows between his back and the headboard. He placed the book of drawings on his bent knees and critiqued the work.

The sketch of Fauna superimposed over the spider bugged him. The image didn't fit. He tore off the paper, balled it up, and sent it sailing to the box in the corner that served as a trash can. He'd have to think about what worked better the next time he drew Fauna.

He smiled and thought about a cooking theme.

CHAPTER 6

Both Anita and Connie were thrilled when I announced I was going to buy the diner. I called the real estate agent to make sure we would meet before I left Asheville.

The drive was beautiful. Summer in western North Carolina was an artist's dream. Vivid blue skies soared overhead, and deep green forests covered towering mountains dusted with wisps of white clouds that made them look like smoke was rising from the ridges. A sense of peace came over me, almost like I was coming home at the end of a long journey.

I pulled off the highway and drove into the small town of Bryson City. Tourism was probably the biggest industry here. The Great Smoky Mountain Railroad depot was right there, with several shops and eateries. Rafting centers were scattered around the town, offering trips down the sedate Tuckasegee River or the wilder Nantahala and Ocoee Rivers. Hiking trails, horseback riding, camping—any outdoor activity you could wish for was close by. Not too far away was the town of Cherokee, which sported the outdoor drama *Unto These Hills*, historic museums, stores of Native Americans artisans, and Harrah's Casino. Any restaurant should do a bang-up business this time of year.

I peered through the dirty windows of the diner I was going to buy. The first sight had me ready to get back in my car and drive away. Fast.

The building had been a bank at one time in the early 1900s and was converted to a diner in the '60s. I think that's the last time it had any updates. Silver duct tape held together the cracked red vinyl of the booths lining the dingy gray walls. Chips and scratches covered the lopsided Formica and metal tables. One dining room chair was missing its seat entirely. A row of mushroom-shaped stools were bolted to the floor in front of a long serving counter. Dust covered everything.

"Hi, you must be Fauna. I'm Cathy Hartfield, Miz Mae's realtor. Or rather the family realtor," said the pretty blonde woman in a rose-colored business suit who appeared next to me. Her pained expression when she glanced through the window told me she knew the condition of the diner. "I know it looks rough, but a good coat of paint and some new furnishings will do wonders."

She opened the lockbox, and we went inside. An old musty smell blessed my nostrils as I walked into the interior. The walls might have been white at one time, but half the plaster had cracked and crumbled off, revealing the same red brick as the front of the building. Scattered mouse turds decorated the dusty serving counter, and a few outdated machines sat on the back work area. An old commercial popcorn popper with a broken glass front, a milkshake mixer that showed rust stains, a coffee maker with three dirty round pots, a hot dog roller oven full of hardened fat splotches—everywhere I looked I saw neglect.

"It's pretty shocking, I know, but don't judge until you see the kitchen." Cathy's voice had a ring of desperation. I swear I heard her thoughts of *"Please buy this shithole and get it off my plate before I go totally insane with this listing."*

The kitchen was a surprise compared to the condition of the dining room. Someone had taken care to prepare this place for a permanent close. The grill and gas stovetop were covered in dust and more mouse leavings, but the overhead vents were clean of petrified grease. No rancid oil congealed in the deep fat fryers, and the oven interior was clear. The equipment was from a top-notch company and appeared to be new. I assumed the owner modernized before the place closed.

This was something I could handle. A glimmer of hope at last.

Still, getting this restaurant idea off the ground would be a tremendous job and a huge risk.

Cathy kept chattering on about the place. "Miz Mae owned and ran this diner until about five years ago, when she turned eighty-one and had to go into the nursing home. She had a bad fall and broke her hip, you see, and she never healed right or else she'd be here right now, scrambling eggs and making toast. She passed last year, and neither of her sons wants to keep the place. They don't live 'round here anyway."

I opened the walk-in refrigerator. Both that and the freezer had been turned off for years. They had that sour shut-in odor to them, but the walls and shelves were mold free. "Do these still work?"

Cathy checked her notes. "They should. Most of the kitchen stuff was purchased and installed just prior to Miz Mae's accident. She did a breakfast and deli lunch only. Lord, I can still taste the blueberry pancakes she made."

If I bought the place, breakfast wouldn't be

served. Most hotels had their own version of a complimentary breakfast included in the room price, and I wasn't about to compete with that.

For fuck's sake, I'm already developing a plan.

"The floor above us has an efficiency apartment that comes with the property. Miz Mae used to let it out for summer help or vacation people. Furniture is gone, though."

That please-buy-this tone sounded in Cathy's voice again. I wondered how long this place had been on the market and how far the brothers would negotiate. My mind ran through budget numbers, costs for redoing the dining area, taking out the soda counter and putting in a bar, repairing and painting the walls, new booths, tables, chairs, stools, linens, a podium and counter for front of house, basic supplies for the kitchen, hiring servers, and a million other things that it would take to make this work. Overwhelming was an understatement to the list of tasks that applied to a project of this magnitude. At least the kitchen only needed a good scrubbing and not updating.

"How much is the asking price?" I turned to Cathy and noted her pained expression. She told me, and I nearly had an aneurysm. "Seriously? Do those men think this place is plated in twenty-four-karat gold?"

Cathy bit her pink lower lip. "I know it's high; however, I'm sure I can talk them down to something more reasonable. That is if you're interested."

I looked at the soda counter and imagined a shining brass and wood bar with classic stools. Shelves of matching dark wood with backing mirrors that displayed top-shelf liquors, local wines, local beer on tap, and a big flat-screen TV on the wall. I'd need a bartender as well. My mental investment estimate went up and my offer went down.

"There's a huge amount of work that needs to be done to get this place functional. I'll have to think about it."

I already knew what I was going to do. If the owners played ball with me, Smoky Mountain Bistro was about to be born.

CHAPTER 7

DODGE CLOSED THE HOOD OF THE BUICK AND WIPED HIS hands on a shop rag. The job was a simple tune-up and replacement of the timing belt. Not his favorite work to do, but two of the regular mechanics called in sick today, and Brick didn't want the everyday repairs to fall behind. His main role at the shop was custom work and paint jobs, but he filled in from time to time. Dodge left the GTO restoration he had going and spent the morning in the main bays, doing oil changes and tire rotations. Dirty and repetitive work, but the money was good, and Brick needed his help. After what the old man had done for him in his life, a few hours of grunt labor wasn't much to ask.

As if on cue, Brick came into the bay carrying a plastic grocery bag. "Dodge, what the hell is kale?"

"Some kind of lettuce, I think. Why?"

Brick pulled out a plastic container and popped off the lid. "Betsey's been on this health kick for a while. She's got a whole mess of green shit in the fridge up at the Lair. Supposed to make me more regular. Don't know why she thinks I need it. This shit gives me the runs."

Bright green leaves, cucumbers, and cherry tomatoes filled the bowl. Brick grimaced. "Only way I can eat this shit is to dump half a bottle of ranch dressing on it."

"Kinda defeats the healthy part of it, right?"

Brick contemplated the salad. "I gotta choke down more of this mess tonight for dinner. Least there'll be chicken or somethin'. God help me if she gets a wild hair and goes vegetarian." He upended the container and dumped the greens into an open trash can. "Come on. Let's go get a burger down at Jimmy Mac's, and don't you breathe a word to Betsey 'bout this."

Dodge grinned and walked to the shop sink to wash his hands. He squirted orange Go-Jo into his palms and worked the gritty lather between his fingers. "That's some pretty strong blackmail material you just handed me."

"I'll lie like a dog and tell her it was your idea."

Dodge laughed out loud. The paper towel roll was empty, so he shook his hands dry and wiped them on the cleanest spot of his work pants. "You told me once you ain't never lied to that woman since you met her."

"I ain't never had to eat no damn kale either."

The two men left the garage bay with a wave to another mechanic and mounted their bikes. The ride to the popular restaurant was only a few minutes. They parked on the street and went inside. Summer tourists filled the place with noise. Harried parents in shorts and sunscreen desperately tried to corral their excited children. Two waitresses lifted huge round trays above their heads to avoid the pinballing bodies.

"Might have been a mistake coming here. It's gonna take forever for a table to open up."

Brick grunted at Dodge's comment. "Tourists. Pain in the ass, but gotta have 'em."

A miracle occurred, and a small table for two cleared in the far back corner of the crowded dining room. The two men sat, but neither of them picked up the menu. They already knew the offerings of the burger joint.

A tired-looking waitress came over to them. "Good afternoon, y'all. What can I get for you?"

Dodge grinned. "Hey, Katie Grace. My friend here wants your biggest kale salad."

The cute blonde wrinkled her nose at Brick. "Kale? We use that stuff as garnish on the plates."

Brick made a growling noise in his throat. "Burger with the works, onion rings, and a sweet tea." He pointed a thick index finger at Dodge. "You mention kale again, I'm takin' your patch."

Dodge didn't attempt to hide his amusement as he grinned at his boss. "I'll have the same."

The perky waitress sauntered off to put in the order.

Brick leaned back and the plastic chair creaked under him. "How's the Goat comin'?"

Dodge sighed. "Slow. Tom's got the engine torn down but told me he's having trouble finding parts. Probably have to use some after-markets. Bill and I started the frame off. I'm thinking candy-apple red."

"Custom?"

Dodge shook his head. "Nope. Keep it classic."

Brick grunted. "Good idea. Like it. What about the Karmen Ghia?"

"Starting on that one after the Goat."

Katie Grace came back and placed two tall red plastic cups in front of them. "Food will be up in a minute."

Her smile lingered on Dodge before a woman yelled that her kid just spilled his juice all over the floor.

"Little young for you, ain't she?" Brick asked once she was gone.

Dodge shrugged. "Out of high school and above the age of eighteen, so technically no, but she's more like my little sister. I've got too much going on for dating anyway."

"Heard Mallory is back."

Brick's gruff words stiffened Dodge's back. "She's in a tough spot. I'm just helping her out."

"She's been in a lot of tough spots."

Dodge had nothing to add. Brick was right. Mallory had been in many bad situations over the years, drifting in and out of his life with regular chaos. First she was the neighbor, then the girlfriend, then the lover, and finally the wife. But in between those titles, she also became the liar, the cheater, the moocher, and the thief.

He still took her back every time. Perhaps he felt sorry for her, as he had firsthand knowledge of the shit show she grew up in, but at what point did a person stop milking their life's sob story and stand on their own two feet?

Not today, apparently.

Brick plucked a napkin from the dispenser and ran it over the table. "I ain't your daddy to tell you what to do. You're a grown man. You got the right to make your own decisions and live by the consequences. Betsey ain't too happy 'bout Mallory, but we got your back. Always will."

Dodge gave a nod to the older man as their food arrived.

The Dragon Runners MC had saved Dodge from the path he trod years ago. His mother left the family before he formed any lasting memories of her. That left him and his father to coexist in a household devoid of love. Sure, Dodge got the basics—food, a bed, clothes, school supplies—but that was it. His dad didn't spend time helping him with homework, conversing about sports, attending school functions or games. Boyer Plott's life composed of work at the Fed-Ex warehouse, then home to eat a frozen microwave dinner and watch TV until bedtime. Dodge played football throughout middle and high school, and not once did his father attend a game. They never took vacation trips to the beach, or Disney World, or anywhere for that matter.

Dodge had two bright spots in his childhood and teenage years. One was his art. He was never happier as a kid than when he had a new sketchbook and colored pencils. Pages and pages of cartoons, super-heroes, mountain landscapes, the river, robots, and more flowed from his fingers to the paper. His favorite subject to draw was the motorcycles that roared up and down the roads, and their riders. He drew elaborate fantasy bikes with huge wheels riding through flames or skimming over water.

He'd met Brick for the first time when he was twelve. His dad was getting a haircut at the barbershop, and Dodge waited outside on a bench with his ever-present sketch pad in his hands. He'd been working on a motorcycle he'd drawn from his imagination, superimposing the picture over a dragon with an elongated head, large wings in full flight, and spewing flames. A shadow had fallen over his book, and Dodge looked up to see Brick standing over him.

Even as a child, Dodge knew who Brick was and about the Dragon Runners MC. There was a healthy amount of fear they generated, but not once had he seen anything but respect in the eyes of the townsfolk for the biker club. Rumors around school were they helped keep the small mountain city clean of drugs and they had enough businesses to employ many people.

"That's some talent you got there. Great fire details. That'd be a really cool custom job on the side of my Harley. Come see me for a job when you get old enough to work."

Dodge's passion was born that day, along with his goal of becoming a Dragon Runner.

Then there was Mallory. She and her mother, Sylvie, moved into the cookie-cutter two-bedroom house next to the one Dodge and his father occupied. At first, Dodge thought Sylvie was sweet on his dad, but if she was, it didn't last long. A rotating string of men lived in that house over the years. Seven of them became "husbands," but Dodge never heard or saw a wedding. Most of them stayed a while and left. It was always obvious when Sylvie had a new man, as Mallory would frequently spend her days outside the house. Dodge stepped in often, taking care of the young girl. Sylvie and husband number eight moved away shortly after Mallory turned eighteen. The girl was left on her own, and that was when Dodge stepped in permanently.

He'd been stepping in ever since.

Brick interrupted his thoughts as two brimming plates were placed in front of them. "Betsey's doin' a barbecue this weekend. You got a show somewhere?"

Dodge shook his head. "Nope. Not until AMA Vintage Motorcycle Days in July. Mute and Stud are going early to set up the display, but I don't think Kat and Eva are gonna be there."

Brick grunted and bit into an onion ring. "Mute will go as long as Kat is okay. Baby number two is comin' soon."

"I'm surprised Eva isn't for a change. How many do she and Stud have now?"

Brick grimaced at the taste in his mouth. He

reached for another napkin and spit the mess out, folding it away. "Ugh. Too much salt even for me. They got five now. All girls. Stud keeps saying they'll keep going until they get a boy. I'd say he needs to quit before he ends up with his own softball team. I can't imagine the dental bill for all them braces."

Dodge chuckled. As perfect as Stud and Eva were physically, he doubted the girls would ever need braces, but again, Brick was right. Kids were expensive. He remembered how much his father complained about the cost of everything. Even now, during one of his sporadic visits to his only remaining parent, Dodge would get an earful of how expensive gas, food, and electricity had become.

A slim hand appeared and snatched a fried ring from his plate. Dodge glanced up to see Mallory standing next to him. She leaned in to press her hip against his shoulder and place her arm over his back. "Hey, baby. Hey, Brick."

Dodge wished like hell he'd seen her come in so he could have prepared himself and maybe avoided her touch. It had been about a month since she showed up at his doorstep and had gotten comfortable being with him. He spent most of his nights at the Lair to avoid her advances, but he had to admit it was kinda nice having someone to come home to again.

The older man gave a short nod. "Mallory." He didn't sound rude, but his unsmiling face had no friendly aura either.

Mallory straightened a bit. "I'm out looking for jobs again. You know any?"

Brick tried another onion ring and frowned at that one, too, but kept chewing.

"Ask Katie Grace if Jimmy has openings," Dodge finally said to fill the silence and answer her question.

She wrinkled her nose. "A waitress?"

"Nothing wrong with being a waitress. My Betsey did that for years." Brick didn't look up as he spoke. Dodge recognized the hardness in his voice. Brick was one of those people who didn't have to shout or erupt and spew anger to get his point across. His authority rang in simple vocal inflections, and very few ever questioned or argued with him.

Mallory, to her credit, recognized her flub and backtracked. "Um… yeah, I'll check with… who was it? Katie Grace?"

"You do that."

Dodge didn't have to be clairvoyant to sense the tension at the table. "Mallie, we need to finish up and get back to the garage. There's a lot of Help Wanted signs all over town. I'm sure you can find something."

"Thanks, baby." She leaned in and kissed Dodge on the temple.

He wished like hell she hadn't done that, but he didn't lean away from her either. It wasn't exactly painful, but he could tell the beginning pull of two different directions. Brick said nothing.

They finished their food, and Brick slipped his card to pay while Dodge left a generous cash tip.

Mallory left the restaurant without talking to anyone.

CHAPTER 8

I heaved another load of trash into the dumpster and wiped my brow. At this rate I'd be lucky to open by the end of summer—three years from now.

Getting a business loan on my own had proved to be a bigger challenge than I expected. I had no assets or collateral other than my car. My trust fund wasn't completely under my control, and even though I could pull a substantial amount from it, there still wasn't quite enough to do what I envisioned, but I had to start somewhere. I made the quick decision to live in the apartment over the restaurant and deal with those conditions later. My focus and energy had to be on the bistro and getting it open by the fall season.

Furnishing the inside came first. I needed to make over the place to fit the upscale image I wanted, but on a tighter budget. The plaster from the bricks was so far gone, it was easier to just crack it all off and skim it with new grouting. Most of the freestanding tables wobbled and were so worn and outdated they had to be replaced. I found some deals online for used restaurant equipment, but there was still a price tag attached. One way to get decor for the place was to hook up with some local artists and work a deal that they would hang their pieces for sale on the walls. That's one expense I would avoid, at least for now.

The kitchen had most of what I needed. Some of the equipment I'd have to adapt to using, then add the ones I wanted later. The biggest problem was the front counter. It had to go. I wanted that space for a smaller finished bar with nice backed stools and a small raised stage in front of the window. Local musicians usually wanted to be paid up front, but there were some who would come play for tips. At least I hoped so. I could do more later, but all of these pieces would have to come in the future, when I had business revenue coming in.

First impressions would get people in the door, but the food and good service would bring them back. I'd have to hire waitstaff and a competent bartender.

I sighed and stretched my neck. My head was full

of what this place could be for me, but my eyes only saw dollar signs. Lots of dollar signs that were on their way out instead of in. It was overwhelming, and the easier road would be to admit defeat now and cut my losses. But that wasn't in my nature, and I'd be damned if I quit before I even got started.

"I remember Miz Mae behind the counter. Lord have mercy, she was a pill to deal with, wasn't she?"

I cocked my head. Someone had come in the dining room of the restaurant. Female from the voice and very Southern.

I hurried back through the kitchen and saw three women standing in the middle of the scrappy room, gazing at the half-done walls and the debris scattered over the floor.

The leader of the group seemed to be the one with the bright red hair. She turned to me with a huge smile that showed lots of white teeth. "Hey there! You must be the new owner. I'm Betsey. This is Molly and Tambre." She stuck out her red-taloned hand for me to shake.

"Fauna Somers."

All three were older, middle-aged I supposed, but obviously none of them got the dress code. Betsey had on leggings and high-heeled boots. *Boots in the summer?* Her green sleeveless blouse shimmered a bit with shots of glittery threads through the bit of fabric that peeked out under the vest she wore. In fact, all three of them wore the same vest. Must be part of the local version of junior league, but I didn't get the country club vibe from them.

"Fauna. That's such a pretty name. So nice to meet you. We wanted to see who ended up buying this place. I thought about it, but we already have an ice cream shop around here, and further down is Psalm's place. Have you been there yet? Soap-n-stuff? She's got the best hair products ever."

I did my best to hide my quick irritation. As a mixed Black and White woman, my hair was a big deal. As a child, my mom spent hours putting chemicals on my head and using a hot ceramic straightener to make my hair "presentable." I have memories of that instrument of torture burning my neck and the tips of my ears. I let my hair go natural now in its state of long corkscrew curls. Easier to maintain, and frankly, I just didn't want to take the time to mess with it. I held the mass back either with a giant clip or a headband, as I did now.

Tambre spoke up in a soft alto. "I have a salon a few streets over. Hair, nails, facials, waxing—all the things for ladies to treat themselves a little."

I admitted I liked Tambre's serene appearance. Something about her was calming and relaxing. She had long, shining dark hair with beautiful silver accents and a glowing skin tone. I didn't know if it was natural or intended, but the effect was stunning. I thought there might have been some Native American blood in her.

Betsey started speaking again, and my easing attitude burred up.

"Our main place is the River's Edge Bar, 'bout ten miles or so down the road."

I put a tight smile on my face and prepared for claws to come out. "Checking out the competition?"

Betsey burst into laughter. "Competition? Lord have mercy, no. From what I've heard, you're puttin' in a swanky upscale restaurant. Our bar is just that— a bar with a little bit of bar food. I sling a little booze and a lot of beer. Nothin' like what's happenin' here. I can't wait to see what you do with it."

Tambre's eyes were on the half-finished walls. "Are you doing all this yourself?" Her voice was quieter, but something about it made you want to listen.

I pushed my headband back from where it had slipped over my forehead. "Yes, I am. The renovation budget is tight, so I have to put in some sweat equity." My shoulders came up in a matter-of-fact shrug. "The more I can do myself, the more I have for investing in the place."

Molly bobbed her head. "Makes perfect sense to

me, but damn, that's a lot of work for one person. You got anyone to help you?"

It hit me then, and I had to swallow. "No, I'm working alone."

It was true. I was alone. My mom had a massive amount of disdain for my chosen field, and neither she nor anyone in my family made any offer to help me. I didn't have the money to hire a big crew, just a few handymen to come in for the jobs I couldn't do myself. Currently, my tiny apartment had a card table, folding chair, and an air mattress because I didn't want to spend money on a bed.

"Pssssht!" Betsey flicked her nails at me. "That just ain't right. You need some extra hands in here, bad." She turned to Tambre. "How full is the garage and the campground? Think we can send a couple prospects down a couple times a week for the heavy stuff?"

"Weatherman is pretty busy ever since his mama got sick. Might could get Forge or Printer."

Betsey frowned. "Printer isn't very reliable. Brick's not sure he's gonna make it to patchin'. I ain't sendin' someone down to help unless they're gonna do it. Rafter might help if he's not on the river."

Weatherman? Forge? Printer? What kind of people name their kids from TV ads?

Betsey turned back to me. "Have you thought about investors?"

My mouth tightened. So that was it. Local bigwigs coming in to offer money and eventually take over. Nope. Not happening. "Thank you for thinking of me, but I'm not interested in taking on investors. I don't really want your hired help either."

If my icy tone had any effect on the woman, it didn't show. She smiled brightly and nodded. "I get that. There's somethin' real satisfyin' 'bout doin' stuff for yourself. We've all been there, but I'll tell you straight up, ain't no strings attached to my offer. My first job was working in a restaurant. An old diner owned by Moses Williams, God rest his soul. My daddy took my pay every week, and I had to squirrel away a little at a time, hopin' one day I could leave this town and find better. I didn't leave, but I did find better. So much better. I look at that as my obligation to pass on my blessings to people who need them the most." She looked around at the bare diner walls. "I think you qualify, Fauna."

My belly quivered with an unexpected warmth. My own mother flatly refused to have anything to do with me or my dreams of building my restaurant, but here was a stranger, offering to help me with no expectations. Yeah, I was skeptical, but the question popped in my brain: Did kind people like this really exist?

My mind flashed to a gorgeous male ass and beautiful back tattoo. Dodge had been kind during a moment when he could have taken advantage of me. The night I got so stinking drunk might have gone very differently if he hadn't been there. I still wondered from time to time where he was and what might have happened should we have stayed in contact.

The buzz of the cell phone in my back pocket interrupted my thoughts. "I'm sorry, but I need to take this."

Betsey winked at me. "No problem, darlin'. Let me know if you change your mind, but whatever you decide, come on down to the bar and I'll buy you a beer. Or two."

They walked out just as I turned away and answered the phone. "What's up, Macie?"

"You can call me your fairy godmother," his excited voice replied. "Or just fairy. Or just godmother. I don't care. I found the motherlode! You know the O'Charley's my friend Burgess has been serving at for so long? Girl, I knew there was something fishy going on. They just announced they've gone belly up, sold the place lock, stock, and barrel. The new owner is gutting everything and making it into a lamp and shade store of all things. The tables, chairs, and booths are getting ripped out and tossed in the trash this weekend. I've already filled up my trunk for you with dishes and kitchen stuff, and I'll get another load tomorrow. Wanna go dumpster diving with me?"

My heart started beating like crazy at the possibility of saving a small fortune. "Is that legal?"

"I don't see why not. They're throwing it all out, and I doubt they care who comes and hauls it off."

As long as the furnishings were in good shape, that would be such an advantage. O'Charley's was a lot bigger than this place, so I could pick through and get the best stuff. That would save me thousands in start-up costs. I'd need a U-Haul truck, one of the big ones, and probably some boxes, packing blankets, and…

Shit, I was going to need bodies too. There was no way I could lift and move that much stuff by myself.

An idea formed in my head. "What's the best time frame?"

"The Lamp King has people coming on Monday morning, so everything has to be out by Thursday, but those big dumpster things won't be in place until Saturday afternoon. You'll have all day Friday, as no one will be on the premises but me and whoever else wants to rummage through the stuff."

"I'll figure something out and see you Thursday. This is so great, Macie. You do not know how much this means to me."

"Just remember me when you start hiring for real. I love my place here in Asheville, but it's getting a little too crowded for comfort."

"Terence again?"

He sighed. "You got that in one, girlfriend. He's been swappin' spit with Juan at the club. Now you know I like me some kink now and then, but three-somes ain't happenin'."

"I hear you. Listen, I'll make arrangements and text you a time frame. Deal?"

"You got it. Best thing you ever did was cut Chase loose. Proud of you, Fauna."

At least one person in my life was happy for me. "Thanks, Macie. You're the best."

I clicked off and rushed to the door, but the three ladies had vanished. No matter.

The River's Edge, eh? I'd finish my day, then take a much-needed shower and put on some nicer clothes. Later tonight I'd head over to the bar and see if Betsey's offer was a real one.

CHAPTER 9

Dodge pulled off onto the dirt-and-gravel driveway leading to an old box house that sat in view of the railroad tracks. The workday in the garage dragged forever, and he was restless from the monotonous jobs. They were still shorthanded, and he had once again spent the day running oil changes, tires, and several brake disc replacements. Everyday ordinary work he could do in his sleep. His original plans were to work on the Goat this evening with the new parts that had come in, but right now, he had his dad to deal with, and even if he was tired as hell, putting it off would make it worse.

As a child, he used to think of where he grew up as a treasure hunter's dream. Now it just looked sad. The front yard was full of old car and motorcycle parts, slowly rusting and decaying into the dust. Just like the man who lived there.

Boyer Plott came out of the building and down the three uneven porch steps to sit in a small area with a blackened firepit and two folding camp chairs.

Dodge dismounted and kicked down the stand. He hated bringing his bike to this dusty place, but it couldn't be helped. *Dirt washes off,* he told himself, as he had many times in his life.

"Hey, Pop."

The older man squinted up at his son. "Want a beer?"

Dodge shook his head. "Not now. I have stuff to do later."

The man grunted. "Ain't been here in a while."

"I've been busy."

"Too busy to come see your old man, I guess."

Dodge bit down on his lip. His father had a lot of practice throwing tiny guilt-trip barbs over the years. Dodge thought he'd grown immune to it, but those little darts added up, and he could still feel the sting.

Boyer dropped his eyes to his hands and picked at the dry cuticles. "Been texting you all day. Cain't even get a reply."

"I replied a couple of times. I told you I was working in the main garage and I'd come see you as soon as I finished."

"I needed help here too. Guess I ain't as important as your friends."

There it was again. Dodge clamped down on his patience. "What do you need, Pop?"

The seated man jerked his chin to a corner of the scrappy yard. "Got them logs over yonder needs stackin'."

Busy work. Move this pile of leaves from one end of the property to the other. Fix the sticking empty drawer in the kitchen that never gets used. Pick up all those twigs that fall in the front yard between the scattered engines and car parts. It didn't take a genius to figure out that Boyer made up work just to get Dodge to come home. The man was a stubborn old goat, but he was also a lonely one.

"I can help you get the wood pile in order." Dodge ignored his aching back. He'd soak it with a nice long shower once he finally got home. "You ate dinner yet?"

"I'll just heat me up a TV tray or a can a' soup. No need to cook a meal for one."

"Soup ain't food. I'll take you to town for a burger after I get the logs stacked."

"Mighty nice, but I'll just stay here in case someone comes to visit."

Another sting pricked Dodge's heart. Seldom did his father leave the dilapidated house and junky yard. He made extra money buying and selling parts he salvaged during the few trips he did make, but for the most part, Boyer's world consisted of this tiny space. Dodge grew up going to school, playing football, displaying his art, and ultimately joining the Dragon Runners MC, all without his father's blessing or participation.

Still, this man was his dad and needed the care of his son. "When was the last time you had a steak? I'll run down to Ingles and grab a couple of rib eyes. After the work gets done, we'll fire up the grill. Sound good?"

Boyer harrumphed and spat on the ground. "Might be nice havin' a decent meal for a change." The older man heaved his body up, and Dodge noted the slow movements. "Time's a'wastin'."

A third sting lanced Dodge's heart. How often had he heard those exact words as he grew up? This was Boyer's favorite way of ending a conversation. "Sure, Pop." Dodge hesitated before sharing the news. "Mallory's back. Staying with me for now while she's looking for work."

The older man didn't stop his forward motion. "Best not spend your money on rib eyes. Hamburger meat is good enough for me."

THE JOB WAS A SHORT ONE, BUT AFTER THE LONG DAY AT the garage, Dodge's energy waned quickly. In the end, his father reduced dinner to scrambling the last of the eggs he had in the refrigerator.

Dodge got on his bike. Through the curtainless window, he saw Boyer lean back in his worn recliner and flick on the TV. No wave or send-off, just a half-hearted goodbye. Dodge shook his head and wondered if his father even thought about him other than when he needed or wanted help.

Restlessness bubbled up in his gut. Running the Tail helped when he had the need to move, but fatigue and a curving twisted road were a bad combination. Too many people had been seriously hurt and some had lost lives because of making bad choices on the backs of their motorcycles. The problem was he didn't want to go home yet. Not tonight.

He made a decision and plopped the helmet on his head. His brothers would be at the River's Edge Bar this time of night, and he suddenly had the need to be around people who appreciated him.

CHAPTER 10

The River's Edge Bar was a surprise. I wasn't sure what I'd expected, but this wasn't it. The building was long and clean with a big stone chimney at one end, reminiscent of a giant log cabin. An open porch invited you to sit on several long benches that looked like split finished logs. I recognized chainsaw art when I saw it. A row of motorcycles lined up along the front of the building, and behind it, I glimpsed the moving water of the Nantahala River.

I sighed. This was the perfect spot for a bar restaurant, and I couldn't help but envy the location. True, it wasn't in town, but it was still off a main highway and easily accessible with plenty of parking space. This far out, I was sure noise wasn't a problem, as there were no residential areas and only a few scattered houses along the road.

I stood in the gravel lot and stared for a few moments to gather my courage. Never in my life had I been in a biker bar. The closest I came to that culture was when I met Dodge so many weeks ago. The man still burned in my mind with his blond hair and fantastic body.

I shook my head to clear it. "Get it together, girl," I said aloud to myself. "Gotta swallow a little pride, but it'll taste better once you have your restaurant up and running."

The volume of music and conversation hit me when I opened the door and walked in. It was early on a weeknight, but the crowd was still impressive. People lined up at the bar, and several tables were occupied. I bet they packed this place on weekends.

A server in jean shorts, a black bedazzled tank top, and boots sauntered by with a round tray in her hand. Her heavily made-up eyes darted to me, and then she stopped and stared with a cocked eyebrow. I had no illusions why.

A sea of White male faces turned to look at me, the oddball newcomer. This was not the first time I'd been the only Black female in the room. Hell, it wasn't the first time I'd been one of few women around period. Most of my professional life had been that way, considering culinary school was still mostly male dominated, but I couldn't say I was used to it.

My heart sped up and my feet urged me to turn around and leave; however, I needed this favor that woman Betsey promised. She said I could come by anytime. Best-case, she was here and I could talk to her. Worst-case, I just embarrassed the shit out of myself and would have to figure out another way to get the restaurant furniture to my place. Nope, scratch that. Worst-case would be asking my parents for help again. I'd rather sell a kidney than deal with that scenario.

I cleared the lump in my throat and gathered my best fake confidence. "I'm looking for Bet—"

"Hey! Fauna! Welcome to the River's Edge. I'm so glad you came!"

A redheaded cyclone of energy enveloped me in two arms and full body contact. Every muscle in my body stiffened in shock as I inhaled a light floral perfume. My family didn't hug. Ever.

Thankfully, Betsey didn't notice my lack of return embrace. "Come over to the bar and I'll get that beer for you. Or would you rather have a drink? We don't have much in the way of fancy, but if you can stay awhile, Katrina is supposed to come out for a bit. She makes the most wonderful margaritas. You'll love them!"

I was sure the smile on my face came out awkwardly, but with her grip on my elbow, I had little choice to move away. Betsey babbled away as she pulled me in her wake toward the polished wood.

"I told Psalm about your place, and she's really excited. We got an idea for you if you want, 'bout stuff for your walls. She's got lots of pictures from local people and will work a deal with you about commissioned sales. We can go by the store anytime and check them out. Win-win, right? There's this one painting that shows the mountains coming through the morning mist. It's just gorgeous."

I wondered if Betsey had an extra lung for breath capacity. She never stopped talking.

A behemoth sat at one end of the bar, dark and brooding with wavy black hair and beard. He was handsome and built like a linebacker, but his presence held a note of menace that had me pulling back.

"Oh, don't worry, Fauna. That's just Mute. He's one of my boys and is part owner and bouncer here. Katrina is his wife. Lord have mercy, there's a story there!" Betsey grinned at me as she tugged me along. "They have the cutest little baby girl. Mute wanted another one as soon as possible, but Kat wanted to wait a bit longer. Guess who won that argument?"

We made it to the bar, and I planted myself on a chainsaw art stool that resembled a horse's behind. The antsy feeling I got from meeting Mute lingered, and my back was tense. Something was buzzing in the back of my head, but I had too much on my mind to pay much attention to it. I had a goal I needed to focus on, and any distractions had to go away.

I cleared my throat. "A margarita sounds great, and thanks for talking up the restaurant. I have a long way to go, which is why I'm here. I need your help if that offer is still on the table."

Betsey scooted a similar stool close to me and plopped her rounded ass on it. "I'm glad to help, darlin', as long as it's in my power to do so. Whatcha need?"

I explained my situation of getting the restaurant furniture from Asheville to here. Then I found myself going a step further and telling her how I came to Bryson City in the first place. Why the hell I started regurgitating my life's story to this stranger I'd known for a whole twenty minutes was beyond my understanding, but I shared more with Betsey than I had anyone in a very long time.

She stopped talking and her face grew serious as she listened, occasionally making a "hmm" of understanding punctuated by a "Lord have mercy." The only break was when a pretty pregnant brunette came behind the bar and Betsey smiled at her. This must be Katrina, as two margaritas appeared shortly after.

"That's some story," Betsey remarked as she lifted the ice concoction to her red lips and took a generous sip. "I can't stand cheaters. Sure, my boys aren't monks, and we have some women who come to the Lair for the sole purpose of partying with them, but once they claim an old lady, my boys better keep it straight."

"Lair?"

Betsey waved a hand toward the front of the building and twiddled her long red nails. "It's the Dragon Runners' private clubhouse and my home. The entrance is behind that gate across the main road and up the mountain. Invitation only. My husband, Brick, is up there right now, probably eating stuff he shouldn't and telling stories about old Tail rides. I tell you that man is stubborn as hell. I've been trying to get him to cut back on his salt, but he just keeps piling it on. Even bought some of that salt substitute, but he won't use it. I swear he's pickier than my grandkids."

"Tail?" I sipped my own margarita. Something she said struck a note in me. *Dragon Runners? Where have I heard that before?* Then the lime flavor of a superb drink burst on my tongue and distracted me. "Oh, wow! This is good."

The woman named Katrina blushed at my praise and muttered a shy "Thanks." She was tiny compared to her gargantuan husband. I watched her approach the frowning man and set a large white mug in front of him. He didn't move as she poured coffee into it, but after she set the pot down, Mute reached out a huge paw and tenderly cupped his wife's cheek. His expression morphed from scary biker dude to one of such love and devotion of a depth I'd never seen before. Katrina blossomed under his touch, and her true beauty shone through. I forgot all about dragons and simply watched. It was breathtaking.

I'd grown up in a world where showing any emotions was forbidden. Mom had drilled etiquette and appearances into me from the cradle. My brain roiled a bit as I tried to recall the last time anyone looked at me with any sort of love or care. Chase might have at one time, but that dream shattered the moment I saw him fucking another woman.

Dodge's face swam up behind my eyes. The one who got away had shown me, a total stranger, more concern that my blood family or supposed boyfriend. How would it feel to be touched like that by him?

Betsey's voice bored into my thoughts and brought me back to the present. "The Tail of the Dragon. It's the nickname for a piece of Highway 129 that has a long history with this club. Started out as a way for the Cherokee Nation to avoid relocation and the Trail of Tears. Then it became a way for moonshiners to run between the states and avoid the revenuers. That's part of club history as well. Now the Tail is more of a tourist attraction and a rite of passage for our club members. Ever ridden on a motorcycle?"

My mind flashed to the single experience I'd had with Dodge. I hadn't included that encounter when I was dumping my life's drama on Betsey. "Once. A… friend gave me a ride home on the back of his bike. I thought it was really cool."

Her eyes softened. "It's a big deal for a real biker to allow someone to ride with him. Means he's got respect for you. Usually only old ladies get that honor, so your friend must think a lot of you."

"I doubt I'm gonna see him again. He was a nice guy, but I can safely say he's the one who got away." Those repeated words rang in my head.

Betsey's nails clicked as she tapped two of them against the sweating glass. "Fate has a way of turning things. Who knows? You might run into him again."

In retrospect, I should have paid attention to that buzz. The feeling of seeing a car crash happen or a giant tree topple over or an engulfing wave rush up the beach. Slow disasters that once they start, there's nothing you can do to stop them, and all that's left is to ride it out.

The older woman's eyes glanced behind me and lit up. "I know exactly who can help you get your stuff. He's between shows and has the big trailer we use for transporting cars." She lifted her hand and waved to someone. "Hey, Dodge! Come over here."

DODGE ENTERED THE LOUD BAR IN A BAD MOOD AND was prepared to stay that way. He let out a sigh as the noise washed over him. Music. Laughter. Happy people. Good times. He should probably stop complaining about his circumstances and appreciate what he had going for himself. A job he loved and a club that had his back no matter what. Mallory had that at one time, but when she left him, she left the club too. If she ever became his old lady again, she'd be accepted back only because of him, but he doubted she'd be greeted with a warm welcome. The hurt of her leaving him in the manner she did still burned in his gut. It came back time after time as she'd drifted in and out of his life over the years, and he didn't think he'd ever get over it.

No matter. He was content with his life, if not completely happy. Perhaps that was enough.

The urge for a cigarette hit him, but he tamped it down. He gave up smoking a long time ago, but something about the bar and the atmosphere tonight brought out those cravings. He didn't know why his tension suddenly ramped up. This was the River's Edge, a home away from home. Most people here knew him, and normally he was comfortable walking in the door, but something didn't sit right tonight. Anxiety had his nerves firing on alert, and his fingers were twitchy. He'd had this feeling before of an impending fiasco and had no control to stop it.

It bothered him. A lot.

Probably my houseguest. He glanced around the bar, taking in his friends and club brothers. Mute was in his usual spot. Stud sang into a mic on the stage with his band. Forge danced on the wood floor with several women around him. Table might be in the back room shooting pool, but his wife, Lori, was pregnant again, and they spent more time at home rather than the clubhouse.

Dodge twisted his head to stretch the tight tendons. He just needed to relax and unwind. Yeah, that was it. Just relax and—

"Hey, Dodge! Come over here."

He heard Betsey's summons and saw her waving hands. A white noise started in his ears, drowning out all other sound. Every nerve and cell of his body focused on the woman whose back was to him. A head of tight-curling long black ringlets and an ass that could make a man weep with gratitude.

No. Not here. Not now.

She turned and her laser eyes hit him with enough force he had to step back. Fauna. The woman who haunted his dreams and lived in his fantasy world. The woman in his thoughts while another one slept in his bed. The woman he'd put into the category of "the one who got away" and was supposed to be a fond memory.

Shit! What the fuck is she doing here?

From her expression, she was asking the same question about him. He wondered how he should play this. Ignorance? Walk up and hug her as if they were old friends? Kiss her like crazy and take her straight to his room at the Lair and finish what they started so long ago?

Fuck, Dodge, get it together!

He walked over to the two women, doing his best not to stare. His mouth was dry, and he had to clear his throat several times before speaking. "Hey, Betsey. What's up?"

"This here's Fauna. She just moved to town and is redoing Mae's old diner into a swanky new place. Fauna, this is one of my boys, Dodge."

Her unwavering tawny eyes met his. "Nice to meet you, Dodge." She stuck out her hand in greeting as anyone would when meeting for the first time.

So that's the way she wants it. Okay, I can do that. He smiled and forced himself to relax. "Nice to meet you, too, Fauna." Her hand was firm in his as she pumped it twice before releasing.

Yup, he could do this. Just two people meeting for the first time. Not like he remembered her lithe body as it bowed up when she came under his tongue.

Betsey's voice interrupted his wayward thoughts, and he turned his attention to her. "What was that?"

"There's some furniture and stuff she needs moved from Asheville to here ASAP. I thought if you weren't too busy at the shop for the next few days, you can take the big trailer over there and help her out. Get some of the boys to go too." If Betsey noticed the strain between Dodge and Fauna, she said nothing about it as she made her request.

He cleared his throat again. "Umm… yeah, I can do that. I'll ask Mute and Bruiser for sure since they're big guys and work mostly at night. Maybe Table if he can get away from his tattoo place."

Betsey sipped her margarita and shook her head at the same time. "Lori's about to pop. I don't think he'll want to be away in another city. How 'bout Stud or Rafter?"

"Yeah, sure. At least one of them should be available. Maybe both."

It was Fauna's turn to clear her throat. "I really appreciate the help. Please tell me what I owe you for this."

Betsey wrinkled her nose. "Psshht. We don't charge people for favors, darlin'. If you really want to pay us back, treat us to a good meal when you open up. That's good enough for me. Dodge?"

He couldn't help himself. "As long as you're not serving mussels."

Fauna's lips rolled in as she got his joke. "Nope. Somehow I doubt I'll ever put that on my menus."

Dodge smiled genuinely this time. No harm, no foul, as all he did at their last encounter was act as gentlemanly as he could. What the future held was anyone's guess. Fauna was here in his town and making a go of a new business for herself. Maybe if he got to know her better, became friends—

"Hey, y'all!"

The trilling voice sent ice down his spine and shredded his future plans to confetti. Dodge felt as if a noose had suddenly dropped around his neck. A prickle of pain darted in his heart as the invisible rope tightened.

Fauna's eyes darted to the woman who appeared at his side and pushed her way under his shoulder.

"I'm Mallory."

CHAPTER 11

I watched as Dodge shifted a wide ramp at the back of the giant truck. It clanged loudly as it landed in place. An echo from the empty box trailer amplified the sound in the morning air. I breathed in dampness and was forever grateful I'd made the decision to accept Betsey and Dodge's offer. Four motorcycles drove up to the lot and parked next to the empty restaurant, and I recognized the men I'd met at the bar: Mute, big and silent; Rafter, young and newly accepted into the club; Bruiser, the rotund bartender; and Stud, who resembled a Viking god.

"Is that him?" Macie whispered as he waved his hand at his face. "Good golly, Miss Molly, if that's what real mountain men are supposed to look like, I need to move to your neck of the woods."

Yeah, they were hot. All of them, including

Dodge. I drove to Asheville last night to hang out with Macie and get a look at the abandoned restaurant furnishings. Some of them were damaged, but there was enough there to get my place up and running. The dishes were plain white china, but they were in good shape. Dinner plates, glassware, cutlery, storage units, bar glasses, some odd mixers—almost everything I needed.

Last night, Macie and I made up a game plan for what I needed to salvage and what I had to purchase. Then we proceeded to drink away the night in a long and loud bitch session about men and all their wrongdoings.

"Imma stay single. Too mush fuckin' drama. Doan need it."

"Amen, gurl-fren."

I hadn't intended to tell Macie about my encounter with Dodge, but two bottles of wine had unglued my tongue and my wits. He already knew about my epic breakup with Chase, but when I told him about waking up naked in the hotel room, he laughed at me so hard that he fell off the couch. Then he cracked open a third bottle of wine after I told him about re-meeting Dodge at the bar and then his woman, Mallory. Betsey told me later in a sharp voice that she used to be his old lady. Whatever that was!

"Listen, sunshine. You need to keeb yore head on

straight and do yore own life. No more fuckin' strange men in hotel roomz."

"I didn't fuck 'im. We jus' messed aroun'."

This early morning, Macie got an eyeful of the man as he walked toward us. "If he swung my way, I'd have fucked him."

My face flamed as my head pulsed with a slight hangover. "Quiet, Macie."

"He can't hear me."

"Shut up!"

Apparently, overindulgence with wine didn't affect my friend at all. My hiss fell on deaf ears the way Macie ignored it. "Hey there. You must be Dodge 'cause Fauna described your hotness to a T."

Dodge's face reddened to a similar shade as mine. "Um… thanks. This is pretty big. All of this going in?"

I slapped Macie in the stomach before he could say anything else. My BFF had the annoying tendency to make innuendos anytime it was possible. *Shit, what does that say about me?* "I've tagged the pieces I want. The rest will go in the dumpster some-time tomorrow."

"Okay, then. We'll get started. It shouldn't take too long, and then we can get on the road."

The five men worked together as one unit, lifting, loading, repositioning, and fitting the pieces into the long trailer as if they were playing Tetris. Tables, chairs, booth components, light fixtures, even a front-of-house greeting kiosk and a big box of office supplies.

I noticed Dodge kept getting texts. He'd stop what he was doing and frown at his phone. It could be anybody, but the pricking at the back of my neck told me it was the ex-girlfriend who was bugging him. About what, I didn't know. I might not have cared either except for Dodge's facial expressions. He was not happy at the interruption. He fired off a couple of answers before resuming his lifting and packing. I kept my mouth shut and did my part in moving stuff around.

Somehow, it all worked out. They'd packed the big box full to the ceiling, carefully stacked, with not a square inch of space left. I imagined the weight of the boxy vehicle would make the drive back slower and cumbersome on the mountain roads to Bryson City.

"The guys are finishing up and gonna go get some food before heading back. I'll go on ahead and drive the truck since I know how to handle a load this size."

I ignored the choked-off comment Macie was dying to say and faced Dodge as professionally as possible. "Thanks for all your help. I don't know how

I could have pulled this off without it. Let me know what I can do to repay you."

Macie made another noise, and I contemplated how to murder my best friend.

Dodge, on the other hand, was clueless. "You can feed me sometime after you open up. I'd love to eat at your place."

Macie brayed a huge horse laugh. "I can't stand it! I'm gonna go check the rest of the stuff and see if there's anything else usable. Love you, girlfriend." He gave Dodge his best sexy eye flutter and pursed lips. "You, too, sugar."

"Is your friend all right?" Dodge asked as Macie sauntered off.

"For now," I muttered. "No guarantees later. Can I call you for bail money?"

He grinned and opened his mouth to answer when a car screeched up to the lot. A lead anchor dropped in my stomach as Chase leapt from the interior. His face was hard and angry as he strode toward us. I braced myself for a confrontation. Over what, I had no clue, but his pissed-off demeanor said he was ready to take it out on me.

"You fucking bitch! I lost my job because of your shit!"

Whoa. Fired? "How's that my fault? I haven't been

at the Omni for a couple of months. You've had plenty of time to fuck things up all by yourself."

He threw his hands in the air. "It was your sabotage that did it! No one listened to me, and the lines fell apart night after night. The waitstaff couldn't keep things straight, and some of them quit right after you did. Prep was awful. Food getting cut wrong, cooked wrong, seasoned wrong. The kitchen failed inspection three times in a row because you made such a big deal over the seafood."

My temper flared. "People got sick, you moron! What else was I supposed to do? Let them get food poisoning?"

He slapped his chest with an open hand. "I'm the head chef. It's my kitchen. I'll run it the way I want to!"

"Was," a new low voice growled at my back, sending shivers down my spine. Not ones of fear but of thrill.

Chase blinked at the interruption and looked behind me. Whatever he saw drained the color from his face, going from angry red to scared white. I hazarded a quick glance and that anchor in my stomach relodged itself deep.

I could safely say there was nothing more menacing than five angry bikers decked out in full riding gear. The other Dragon Runners must have heard the shouting and came to take Dodge's back.

Nope. They came to take *my* back.

Wow. Just wow.

Chase blinked. "Excuse me?"

Stud spoke. "The correct tense for that sentence is 'I *was* the head chef.' If you got fired, that's on you."

"How 'bout you step back a bit? Give Fauna a little breathing room, yeah?" Dodge's question was more like an order.

Bruiser, Rafter, and Mute stepped around me like bodyguards and forced Chase to move away. Their triple movements enfolded me like a warm security blanket. I blinked at them in sudden emotion. I couldn't remember the last time someone threw down for me like this. For years, any battles I fought, I did it alone. The idea of someone else, let alone several someone elses, standing beside me was so foreign, I didn't know quite how to process it. I had to admit though, I liked it.

Chase straightened himself up to face his new opponents. I'd give him credit for trying to save face, but when that much pure alpha male testosterone kicked in, escalation was inevitable. "She was the one who complained about shit all the damn time. Nonstop. Condition of the walk-ins never right, wiping down stations every fucking second, bitching about food dates and logs, bitching about communication between the kitchen and the floor. Nothing was ever good enough for her."

Dodge shrugged. "So?"

Chase exploded. "What do you mean, 'so'? Who the fuck are you, anyway?" He finally took in the scavenged parking lot. "What's going on here?"

"Nunya," Dodge replied. "As in nunya business. I think it's time for you to leave."

Chase burred up. "I came here to get some stuff for my new restaurant."

A sinking sensation hit my stomach next to that anchor. "Did you buy the lot?"

His hesitation told me all I needed to know. "Well, no. I just heard about the abandonment and—"

"Too late. We already got it. That is, my new friends and I did." I gestured to the bank of pure male hotness behind me. Was it wrong that I enjoyed saying that sooooo much?

"You can't just take everything! That's stealing!"

"Why not? Like you pointed out, it was abandoned and headed for the landfill. Besides, you planned on taking it too. Why is it stealing for me and not for you?"

He sputtered. "It's... I'm—"

Dodge interrupted. "Babe, we need to roll. I have to get back to Bryson City as soon as possible."

"We" need to roll, not "I." I nodded in his direction and wondered if the train of texts was the reason. Not my problem nor my business, but still that *we* stuck in my head. If I was being honest, the *babe* did too. "I wish we could continue this fascinating conversation, Chase, but *we* have places to be. Ciao!"

I turned, intending to make a dramatic exit. A flash of movement and a gasp of pain had me spinning back.

Dodge had Chase's arm in a twist, forcing my ex to bend over lest his shoulder be wrenched from the socket. Dodge had gone from being antsy for the road to enraged in a heartbeat. "I don't know what you city boys learned in kindergarten, but we country folk were taught to keep our hands to ourselves. You remember that next time you wanna touch somebody, yeah?"

I had nothing to say. My heart was pounding hard. I guessed that Chase had reached out to grab me to make me listen to his angry diatribe, and Dodge had stopped him. Another throwdown for me.

Not gonna lie, this turned me on. Big-time.

Fuck me, I'm in trouble!

Dodge let go of Chase's arm, and my ex stood up and moved awkwardly away. He acted like he wanted to say something but was afraid of riling the biker again. Instead, he glared at me as if everything bad in the world was my fault.

I was so over it.

"He's all finished here, aren't you, Chase?" Macie finally came over to rejoin the group. I could tell he was loving every minute of being there. "These gentlemen need to get back to Bryson City as soon as possible."

The way he breathed *gentlemen* made me want to roll my eyes. I loved Macie with all my heart, but sometimes his constant flirting got him into trouble. I didn't know how these bikers would react to having a gay Black man talk to them like that.

None of them seemed to care, though. Stud laughed out loud. "That's for sure. We should have just enough time to get to the restaurant and unload. I have a lot of paperwork to catch up on. Fauna, have you thought about a POS system?"

"No, I haven't."

"I have a couple of suggestions. Come by the bar later if you can and I'll show them to you. We'll see you there, yeah?"

"Sure."

The Viking god smiled and nodded, then crossed his arms and stared pointedly at Chase. I swear I heard his unspoken question: *"You're still here?"*

Chase cradled his arm as he was put on the spot.

A part of me felt sorry for him, as it was obvious that he was outnumbered. Outmanned, too, as in out*man*ned. I guessed anyone would be when faced with such prime examples of male perfection; however, my pity for him evaporated at his next sentence. He couldn't leave without one last shot.

"You're gonna fail, like you do with everything else in your life." He pointed and spat the words at me as he walked backward to his car.

My rejoinder wasn't exactly eloquent, but I wanted to say something back. "Wanna bet, asshole?"

"Sweetness, he ain't worth the trouble. We gotta get goin'," Dodge said as Chase retreated. "We're gonna unload tonight and be back tomorrow afternoon to help arrange stuff where you want it." He didn't wait for me to answer, just raised a hand in the air, making a twirling motion with a raised finger. "Let's go."

The other four men nodded at each other as they moved toward their bikes.

"See you at the restaurant, yeah?"

God, how I love the color of those eyes! "Yeah. I need to get my car and I'll follow you."

He smiled and squeezed my shoulder before walking over to the huge box truck and climbing in.

Macie clicked his tongue twice. "Girlfriend, I

don't know about your bistro, but there's something definitely cooking in Bryson City."

Dodge climbed the steps to his apartment with heavy, tired feet. His back was sore from all the moving he'd done this morning, then the drive from Asheville to Bryson City. They'd parked the truck near the restaurant and made plans to finish moving in over the weekend. Fauna had worked alongside them, lifting and shifting boxes as they loaded. Her gorgeous eyes had glowed with excitement all day long, and her sweaty face beamed at each piece of equipment like she'd found buried gold. The urge to take her in his arms and kiss her silly grew with the passing hours as they worked. She declared she would treat everyone by cooking a three-course meal after setup. That would be one welcome bright spot in his future.

Mallory's constant texts had been the only distraction. Even the brief encounter with Fauna's asshole ex hadn't been as bad as the constant demand of his phone. He'd thought about turning the damn thing off, but he was waiting to hear from the spider client and had to keep it on.

> Mallory: Where are you?

> Mallory: What time are you coming home?

> Mallory: I need to talk to you.

> Mallory: Why don't you answer me?

He swore each time he answered.

> Dodge: I told you, I'm helping someone out of town for the day.

> Dodge: I don't know.

> Dodge: We'll talk later.

> Dodge: Mallie, I'm busy.

One text came from his father asking about when he could schedule some work on the roof. Dodge started to wonder how much longer his shoulders would stay attached as he was pulled in so many directions.

He entered his dark apartment. He could see the pile of dishes in the sink had grown during the day, but he was too damn tired to wash them. Out of habit, he opened the refrigerator and found real food in there. Mallory must have taken the money he left her and gone grocery shopping. At least that was something nice to see. He picked up his favorite beer and popped off the cap.

When they lived together previously, she had several sporadic bouts of obsessive homemaking and organization. Periods of absolute chaos usually followed where she would let everything fall apart around her. He thought at first it was a mental thing, but he figured out it was her pattern of trying to get something from him. Her thought process of "make him happy so I can have what I want" kind of behavior. He used to fall into that trap, but it didn't take long for him to catch on to the game.

He tipped back the bottle and took a long cold drink. *Why the hell am I letting her stay here again?*

He found her asleep in his bed, the sheets pulled down to show her naked breasts.

He'd told her the night she showed up that he'd let her stay a few days. Those few days had turned into weeks, and there was no sign of her moving out. She'd tried to touch him a number of times, but so far he'd resisted. It bothered him that she'd gone as far as she did the night she showed up at his place. He didn't want to call it an assault, but in essence that's what it was. He felt violated and still did, but he kept that information to himself.

He wasn't sure from her text what she wanted to talk about. Work or money, most likely. The job at the grocery store lasted two weeks before she announced that she'd quit. She found another one at a home improvement center. That one lasted a few days. Same thing with the coffee shop and the book exchange. No explanations other than she didn't like her bosses telling her what to do. Dodge had refrained from saying that's what bosses did. She claimed to be looking again, but no one was hiring. He found that hard to believe since there were plenty of seasonal jobs all over town, but he guessed that word had gotten around that she was unreliable.

Several MC businesses had some spots open. Table was looking for a part-time receptionist at the tattoo parlor, Psalm needed counter help at her store, and Tambre had mentioned sometime back about a chair opening up at her hair salon. Mallory didn't have a cosmetology license, but Dodge offered to help her go to school if that's what she wanted.

"Nope," "Nope," and "Hell no" were the answers he got. She wasn't interested in school or working for any of the Dragon Runners.

"Them people ain't gonna hire me. Never liked me much, and I don't like them. They ain't gonna change their minds this time an' I ain't neither."

She was probably right, he mused. He had no illusions that Mallory had taken advantage of his goodwill. Shit, she probably didn't recognize she did it, but the need to protect and help her was so ingrained in him that he allowed it to happen over and over again. Yeah, he wished like hell he could muster up the balls to kick her out, but until then, he'd keep kicking his own ass. Best for him to spend his time away from home and stay at the garage working overtime or up at the Lair.

His thoughts turned to Fauna. Her ex was a piece of work. Anger flashed through his body as Dodge thought about that accusatory finger in Fauna's face.

"You're gonna fail, like you do with everything else in your life."

Dodge found that hard to believe. The woman he saw at the hotel bar so many weeks ago exuded a strong personality and smart instincts. She wasn't afraid of hard work or getting her hands dirty. Starting a business from scratch in a town you'd never lived in around people you didn't know was very risky, yet she'd taken the bull by the horns and was making a go of it. Everything about her was worthy of admiration, and he wished like hell that he'd get to be a small part of it.

Her words back to her ex echoed in his mind.

"Wanna bet, asshole?"

CHAPTER 12

PEGGY JEAN HARTLESS STRUTTED INTO THE SADDLE UP club in her bright pink fringed boots. Bobby Jessop had broken up with her, and she was sick of his shit. She'd caught him again with Lacie Clodfelter, but instead of begging her forgiveness, he told her he was in love with the other girl and wanted to be with her. This was the same scenario with Sierra Mock, Kathy Carter, and Maggie Phelps.

Not this time! Peggy fumed. Tonight, she was fixin' to dance her ass off and find a new man. A better one. She twitched her rounded behind as she paid her cover charge and entered the club.

Even in this one-horse town, tourists were thick. The club was the biggest draw next to the casino and some other scattered roadside attractions. Some people were there for the big horse stables her grandfather's club owned and operated. Peggy grew up around the large creatures and regarded them as pets rather than working animals.

"Hmph, I'd like that no-count Bobby to meet Vanilla Bean. My girl would buck him off and stomp him good for me," Peggy muttered as she ordered her first beer of the night.

"Hey, sweet thang. You here alone?" a half-drunk cowboy wannabe asked as he approached her with a super smarmy grin on his face.

Tourist, Peggy thought. He wasn't the most handsome man in the world, but he fit her sour mood. "I ain't alone no more." She took his sweaty hand and led him straight to the dance floor.

More beer, more men, more flirting—just more. Peggy danced and drank in a continuous cycle. She caught a glimpse of Bobby and Lacie and shot them both the bird. Another beer found its way to her hand, and she gulped it down.

"Fuck him and fuck her!" *Oops.* She'd said that last part out loud and giggled. She tried to do a pirouette but wobbled and almost fell. The club was hot and getting hotter.

Air. I need air.

Faces blurred as she stumbled to the door. A hand grabbed her elbow as she fell against someone.

"Hello, pretty lady. Do you need some help?"

The voice was singsongy and a bit strange. Not a local nor a Southerner, but then again, she was drunk. *Fuck, how did I get soooo bad?* "I needa go outside ferrah bit."

The man, whoever he was, allowed her to lean on him as he guided her through the crowd. The air was plentiful but still thick with humidity. She tripped, and the man jerked her up.

"Dzorry."

He didn't say anything, just pulled her to the back of the parking lot to a camper van. The inside smelled musty, and the mattress there was one of those thin camper ones. Peggy's brain locked on to that detail, and her anger over Bobby subsided as fear for herself took over. She tried to fight and push the man away, but he was too strong and she was too drunk.

No, she wasn't drunk. All that dancing should have burned through the beers in her system. She'd been drugged.

"Rellllaxxxxx. I'll bbbbbeeeee donnnnnnne soooonnnnnnn."

Peggy whimpered once before the blackness took over.

CHAPTER 13

Brick stared unseeing at the Dragon Runners circling the meeting room conference table. Dodge noted the grim expression on the man's face and the clenching and unclenching of his fists. Something bothered the president of the club, and it showed.

Dodge pinched the bridge of his nose against the headache that bloomed behind his eyes. The weekend had been full of grunt work for his father, and he hadn't had a chance to get back over to Fauna's place to help her like he said he would. Guilt ate at him over it. The other bikers had spent the day after the big acquisition getting everything in their proper places. Rafter texted him a selfie of him and Fauna resting against a random stack of booth pieces, insane grins on their shiny faces.

> Rafter: Missing you, brother. Got it all in. You get to finish installing.

A second pic was a candid one of Fauna cooking some sort of stir-fry on the restaurant's grill.

> Rafter: I don't know what it is, but it sure smells good!

Then a series of pics of Mute, Bruiser, and Stud shoving food in their mouths.

> Rafter: Damn, brother, you're missing out big-time.

That was Saturday while he listened to his father's complaints. The jealousy that smoldered in his gut didn't surprise him but added to the guilty weight on his shoulders.

It didn't help that in between the pics, he received texts from Mallory.

> Mallory: When are you coming home?

> Mallory: I haven't seen you much in a couple days.

> Mallory: I miss you, baby.

Now this emergency Sunday night church meeting with the Dragon Runners. There were a dozen different directions he was being pulled to, and there would be a point when he would rip apart.

Brick didn't waste any time. "I got a call from Colonel yesterday over in Maggie Valley. Said there's been some drug problems in town."

Stud leaned forward and moved his laptop to rest his elbows on the carved table. "The only drug people we know for sure are the Jessop boys. They deal in weed and moonshine, but they know not to sell to kids. We ran the hard shit out of town years ago. Shouldn't be coming back. Is he worried about that in his town?"

Brick shook his head. "I ain't concerned about the Jessops. Henry and I go way back. They make some premium 'shine, but they're real careful about who they deal with. There's some unofficial hard drinkin' spot over there, but as long as it don't come over here, we're good. This is somethin' different. Colonel said no one paid much attention to the first one, but another one got reported last week, and two more girls came forward yesterday."

Dodge dropped his hand, and his chair creaked as he settled himself. "What are you talking about?"

"Some women got roofied and assaulted. Tourists

mostly. They go to that big fancy dance place that has all them whiskey barrels for decorations."

Brick's answer sent a palpable wave of anger around the table. The Dragon Runners weren't perfectly behaved choirboys, but when it came to their women and the women of the community, there were no better protectors.

"How many?" Stud inquired grimly. "And do we need to be concerned about that here?"

"I don't know. Neither does Colonel, but he suspects there's some we ain't heard about. That place does weddings and parties and shit. Take any night of the week and you're apt to find a bunch of women drunk off their asses. I guess it's hard to tell if you're drunk or drugged, but somehow the sheriff over there figured it out." Brick jammed a hand over his craggy face. "Bad enough that shit happened to out-of-towners. Now one of our own got hurt. Little Peg, Colonel's granddaughter, is one of the girls."

"Fuck! Isn't she like twelve or something?" Bruiser turned to a glowering Mute as if he expected an answer.

The big man shook his head and flashed his hands twice, then added one finger.

"Twenty-one? When the hell did she grow up?"

"It happens. I'm amazed every day at my girls and how fast the time has gone." Stud's demeanor turned dark. "If any asshole came after them, there wouldn't be enough pieces of him left to make an identification."

Brick grunted. "I've put a lot of men up the mountain. I'm getting' too old to keep up. Hell, last time I took Betsey over to Asheville for a visit, we went to a restaurant that didn't have menus. Had to take a picture of this black-an'-white computer thing just to find out what they had to eat."

Bruiser raised his brows. "A QR code."

"I don't know what the hell it was. All I know is Betsey had to use her phone, and it was damn hard to read them little words."

"You can make the screen bigger by—"

"I ain't interested in that shit, Bruiser. All that tech mess is what you do, not me. This old dog is tired as hell of learnin' new tricks." The man gave a big sigh. "Seems the world is changing so damn fast, I can't keep up no more. I'm thinkin' it might be time for someone else to lead the Dragon Runners."

Shock replaced the anger as the entire brotherhood absorbed the unexpected announcement. Brick was the man who'd pulled the club back from the brink of extinction and made it into the tight communal group they knew it to be. He spent the majority of his adult life cleaning up after the old guard, developing legit businesses, and balancing between the law and biker justice. The idea of the Dragon Runners MC without Brick as its leader was unthinkable.

Dodge coughed into the silence. "Well, boss man, today you're still sitting at the head of the table. Is Colonel looking for help, or is he just warning us?"

Brick cleared his throat and addressed the room. "He's a proud man and don't want no help. Already put the word out that whoever messed with his granddaughter is a dead man. He thinks it's another tourist who's gone by now. I'm thinkin' our reputation will keep our ladies safe, but not everyone knows us. Best keep a close eye on things."

He raised the gavel and banged it once on the polished round sound block. "Adjourned. Dodge, stick around for a minute."

The rest of the members filed out while conversing about beer and games of pool.

"Mallory's still at your place." The president's words came out not as a question but a statement of fact.

Dodge wished for a painkiller as shards stabbed him behind his eyes. He took in a deep breath through his nose and let it out slowly through pursed lips. "Yeah, she's still there. It's either that or living in her car."

Brick grunted. "I saw you workin' on that piece o'

shit last week. Had to work overtime to keep on schedule with the shop. You gonna be able to make that car show comin' up?"

Dodge stiffened. "I've never let you down, Brick."

"An' you ain't lettin' me down now. Betsey is real concerned about you. She remembers what it was like when Mallory was a part of this club as your old lady."

It was easy to read between the lines. Whenever Brick brought up Betsey's concerns, he really meant his own. Dodge appreciated it, but he was still a bit irritated. "It's no big deal. She'll leave when she gets on her feet. In the meantime, I won't let her affect me at work."

"Work's not the problem. It's unfinished business."

There was a wealth of meaning behind those words. Dodge took another big breath. "Yeah, I know."

He left the church meeting and descended the steps to the main living area of the clubhouse. A few members were shooting pool, and others were playing video games. Donna, a club regular, cleared some empties and tossed them into the big gray trash can set aside specifically for cans and bottles. Rafter leaned on a cue stick and lifted two fingers to flick against his temple as a greeting. Forge gave a quick head jerk as he lined up his next shot.

Normally, he would go join them for a game, but there was a restlessness in his gut. He didn't want to hang here, nor did he want to go home. The sun was finally waning, but it was still light enough for a ride on the Tail. Even that idea didn't settle him.

He left the compound on his bike, carefully making his way down the incline and through the privacy gate. In front of him he saw the light on at the River's Edge, but instead of stopping in to see Mute and Kat, he turned his front wheel in the town's direction.

Unless there was a festival, downtown was usually dead on a Sunday night. The lights in Psalm's place were dark save for the ones at the top where the family lived. He imagined Blue would be reading stories to his kids while Psalm waited for him. Blue was a member of the club, as befitted him for being Brick's son, but he stayed away from a lot of the club businesses. So far, most of the townsfolk were okay with the situation, although a few eyebrows rose from time to time.

Happy man, happy family. After the shit in his life, Blue deserved every bit of it.

Dodge let the bike slowly roll through the empty streets. The depot was closed. So were the ice cream parlor, the bookstore, the coffee shop, and Jimmy's. Even Table's tattoo business was locked up for the night. The only light showing came from the Smoky Mountain Bistro, still in progress.

The pictures Rafter sent him showed the booth components and other furniture piled in their respective places, but they needed to be assembled and installed. There were tables and chairs in pieces, plus boxes upon boxes of dishes, pots, pans, and other kitchen stuff. Fauna had hired out for some of the bigger construction work, but she was determined to do as much as she could herself. He had to admire her grit, but he also recognized her need for help. He could see her through the glass window in the door, pulling at a wall partition that separated booth space. The thing probably weighed more than she did.

His problem was that the more he was around her, the more he wanted to *be* around her. He should give up and go home. Or back to the Lair. Or go on the Tail and clear his head.

His hand lifted as if making up its own mind and knocked on the door. A moment later, a disheveled Fauna clicked open the bolt and let him in. She was panting a little, as if she'd just run a marathon or at least had a long session on a treadmill.

"Hey, Dodge. What are you doing here?"

What am *I doing here?* "Just cruisin' by and saw your light. You're still working, aren't you?"

She smiled. "Yes. I should be tired as hell, but I'm too jazzed up from the weekend. I thought if I keep at it, I'll eventually get myself worn out."

He grunted. "I know the feeling. Mind if I come in for a bit? I can help you move some of the bigger stuff around. Maybe hold up that piece you're wrestling while you screw it in."

She inhaled deep, and her breathing slowed. "Yeah, I could use the help. I owe you a meal in any case. There's a big pot of vegetable soup on the stove and a baguette fresh from the oven if you're hungry. It's nice and thick."

Something let loose in his gut, and he almost grinned at her words. "That sounds great. What do you want to get done tonight?"

"If we get just one booth set up, I'll be happy."

The tools she had weren't very sturdy, and he struggled to get the braces screwed together. It took them over an hour just to get one bench put up and anchored.

"At this rate, we'll finish by Christmas. I'll bring my power tools tomorrow night and this will go a lot faster." He spooned up some of the chunky soup. "This is really good, by the way. Much better than the stuff I get out of the cans."

She swiped some damp tendrils from her forehead. "Canned soup? Please. That's an ingredient, not real food." Her grousing tone had a humorous tinge to it. "I don't want to take up all your free time."

"If it becomes a problem, I'll let you know."

"What about your girlfriend? Won't she be upset?"

The question was valid, but her supposition was wrong. "Mallory is not my girlfriend."

"Ex-wife?"

His back tightened at the question. He was pretty sure she was mining for information, and it became very important to make sure his present relationship with Mallory was as defined as he could make it. "We're not back together, if that's what you think. It's… complicated."

The quiet deepened. Dodge sensed there were unseen landmines—one misstep and something would blow up. "We grew up together," he explained. "Her mom was too busy to be a mom. My dad was around, but he didn't pay a whole lot of attention to me. Anyway, Mallory used to come over to my house every day after school and stayed for dinner most of the time. We did our homework, took our clothes to the laundromat, pretty much lived our lives side by side. We depended on each other all through school, and it seemed the next natural step to get married when we graduated."

Dodge's eyes burned a bit as he pictured the day of his wedding. A simple ceremony at the courthouse with no frills. Just the bride dressed in new jeans and boots and the groom in a Dragon Runners MC cut that declared him to be a prospect. None of it mattered, as all he could see at that time was a beautiful future with the woman he loved and cherished above all. He had no clue back then that it was a smoke-and-mirrors kind of day. Once that ring landed on Mallory's finger, she considered it her ticket to freedom rather than linking herself to him as his wife.

He coughed and cleared his throat. "Long story that's growing longer. I found out the hard way that she needed more than just me to be happy. It's over, and it's been over a long time. I'm helping her out is all."

Fauna nodded and thankfully dropped the touchy subject. "Okay, then. I'll take the help when you have time and feed you. I need to cook some test meals, so you can be my guinea pig."

He popped the last of the warm, crusty bread in his mouth. "You're on. Thanks for this, Fauna. It's what I needed."

She burped lightly. "No problem. I'm finally ready for bed. See you soon, okay?"

He left and stayed outside long enough to hear the click as she locked the door. It was a short ride to his place, and exhaustion was making him a little dizzy.

Mallory met him at the door when he pulled up. "Where you been?"

Dodge looked at her skimpy outfit and full makeup. No doubt she'd been waiting for him. "Church at the Lair and then dropped buy a friend's place for a bit."

"A friend? One of the boys?"

"No one you know."

"A woman?"

He was starting to sway on his feet. Tomorrow morning started another workweek, and by the amount on the scheduling board, overtime might be in the picture. His irritation flared up. "Look, Mallie, I'm tired. I have a long week ahead of me, and I don't want to deal with any shit tonight."

"You sleepin' with her?"

Yes, I did, and it was the best night I've had in a long, long, long time. "You don't get to ask those kinds of questions, now do you?"

At his firm tone, her face morphed from combat mode to conciliatory. "I'm sorry, baby. It's just that being home means a lot, and I want to spend more time with you."

He wanted to debate that, but he was too tired. Taking a deep breath, he did something he'd never done in his life: he put himself first. "I'm taking the bed tonight. You get the couch."

His room showed signs of her occupation—clothes on the floor, bed unmade, pillows scattered. In the bathroom, the sink space had been taken over by makeup bottles and brushes.

He took another breath. Then another. *Nope. Not working this time.*

He strode back out to the main room where Mallie stood in the same place, her arms crossed and a petulant expression on her face. "You want to spend more time with me, how 'bout showin' me you actually give a damn. You don't pay rent or buy food, and your 'few days' was up weeks ago. If you're not workin' somewhere and spendin' your days hanging around here, it would be nice if you'd clean up a little, fix dinner from time to time. I don't think it's asking too much from you to help me out if you're still livin' here."

Her eyes bugged out, and she gasped at his harsh tone. Perhaps he was going overboard a bit, but he was almost at the end of his patience. "Mallie, I've got a lot goin' on at work, and—"

"Okay." The small remorseful voice had a different ring to it.

"Come again?"

She took a ragged breath. "You're right, Dodge. I haven't been helpin' out like I should. You been real good to me, and I ain't never treated you right. It's 'bout time I did since you done so much for me all these years. I cain't make up for all I've put you through in the past, but I can make it up to you in the future. I'll start by sayin' thank you."

Dodge was floored. He couldn't remember if those two words had ever passed through Mallory's lips in regard to him. For years, she came to him asking for money and a place to stay, sometimes crying on his shoulder after a bad breakup. Never had she acknowledged his help with any kind of true gratitude.

She took his silence for consent and moved to wrap her arms around his waist, pressing close. Genuine tears leaked from her eyes as she snuggled into him. "Thank you for putting up with me. Out of all the places I been, there's only one I think about as home. That's here. You may not believe it, but I'm real sorry for all the messed-up shit I handed you. Real sorry. I ain't gonna ask you to do nothing more, but can I just sleep in the bed with you? Just sleep? Only place I ever feel safe is right here in your arms."

Dodge's arms came up automatically to her back. Despite regular meals, she was still way underweight, as indicated by her ribs beneath his fingers.

He closed his eyes as his resolve crumbled, and he regretted the words even as he said them. "Just for tonight."

CHAPTER 14

"Hold right there while I screw it in."

I burst into laughter, and Dodge gave me an exasperated look. "That's the third time tonight you've done that."

"Done what?" I asked in my most innocent-sounding voice.

"Made a sex thing out of something I said." He set the drill on the long screw and, with several quick bursts, drove it into place. He pulled at the booth wall to test its sturdiness. "That should keep it up."

His side-eye at me had me laughing again. "Now you're doing it deliberately," I accused.

The grin that came across his face told me all I needed to know.

This was the third night in a row this week that Dodge had come over after his regular workday to help me in my restaurant. I wouldn't be very far along without his help or his tools. The flimsy Phillips screwdriver I'd bought at Dollar General gave up the ghost the first time I tried to use it. Stripped right out, leaving me cussing like a sailor. Thankfully Dodge showed up with a big box of power tools at just the right time.

We spent some time measuring and planning where everything would go. This was difficult, as we had to keep moving shit around the restaurant to check the placement. Once we finally got stuff where it would fit, we started the installation. I had no clue it would take so long to set up one booth. I did as much as I could during the day, which amounted to getting the kitchen in order, washing and putting away dishes, setting up vendor accounts, and getting all the city paperwork completed for a business license and LLC.

It was overwhelming sometimes, but bit by bit, it was coming together.

Dodge also gave me an excuse to cook since I insisted on feeding him when he came over. I picked up fresh ingredients from the local markets and did some experimenting with new and old recipes. We would eat in the booth we'd just finished as we chatted about anything and everything.

"I like cats fine, but I'd rather have dogs."

"I always wanted a parrot. I thought it would be cool to walk around with one sitting on my shoulder."

"Classic action movies, hands down."

"So, is Die Hard *an action or a Christmas movie?"*

"Coke or Pepsi?"

"Neither. Give me a Sprite."

Night after night, whatever subject hit our brains, we talked about it. Sometimes he'd call me to say he was working late and couldn't come by. We'd still talk on the Bluetooth buds in our ears as we worked in separate places. Our conversations got deeper and deeper.

"Yeah, I vote, but not for any political party. I'd rather pick the person who I think can do the job right. I'm a life-long independent."

"I didn't grow up in a church, but I believe in a higher power."

"Smoked a little weed a few times, but it's not on my 'have to have' list."

"I'm not close to my parents."

"Me neither."

Tonight I fixed a somewhat expensive bouillabaisse that turned into a disaster. I'd never done this French fish stew before and definitely needed to talk with another chef about it. I used too much saffron, an ingredient I wasn't familiar with, and the dish turned an unappealing bright orange. One bite had me spitting it out. The spices were all wrong and the flavor way too strong even for my palate. "I have some leftover chicken parmesan and pasta, but I don't think there's enough for two."

"How 'bout a pizza?" Dodge mouthed around a lump of the stew.

"You're on."

The food arrived along with a little nighttime rain. This wasn't a torrential downpour, but it was significant enough that Dodge stuck around longer than he'd expected to. He ran out long enough to cover his bike with a tarp and came back in soaked to the skin. His hair was plastered to his skull, and he shook it at me like a wet dog.

I laughed at the cold shower but, of course, had to cuss at him. "Oh, you asshole!"

"Come on, Fauna. Give me a big hug."

"You're out of your mind. Get away from me."

"Please, sweetness?"

"No."

He scrunched his face and bulged his eyes.

I circled my fingers at him. "What the hell is that?"

"Puppy dog eyes. Is it working?"

"Not in the least. Don't ever do that again."

Truthfully, this playful side of him was great. As a worker, he took his job seriously. Even more so as a friend and supporter. It was really cool to watch him relax and just have fun. I had the feeling he didn't get a lot of that in his life.

He opened the pizza box, and we dug in.

"Thank God you're not one of those," I said around a mouthful of gooey cheese, limp pepperoni, and so-so sauce. Yeah, this chain store offering wasn't exactly a culinary experience, but at the moment, I was more interested in fuel rather than taste.

"What do you mean?" He took his own gargantuan bite and half the slice disappeared.

"Pineapple. Not on pizza. Pineapple is dessert."

He shrugged and bit into the crust rind. "I don't know. I kinda like a bit of sweet with my savory."

"Sorry, but we can't be friends anymore."

He swallowed and opened his mouth to say something else when his phone buzzed. The change in him was instantaneous, almost like a curtain dropped over him and all the light he'd shone tonight was snuffed out. His mouth turned down as he answered.

A pang hit my own good mood. *Mallory? Probably. Who else would be calling him?*

"Hey, Pop. Everything okay?"

So it wasn't Mallory but his father. Was I a bad person to feel relieved? I didn't mean to eavesdrop, but it was hard not to when Dodge sat only three feet away from me.

"Now? Pop, no store is open at this hour for me to get parts. Just close the shutoff valve and I'll come by tomorrow."

I watched as Dodge pinched the bridge of his nose and closed his eyes. "I've been really busy lately. Overtime at the shop and then helping out a friend with her restaurant. Fauna. No, you don't know her."

He mouthed a cuss word before finishing his conversation. "All right, I'll be there in a bit."

He hung up and raised his tired eyes to me. "Fauna, I need to—"

"That was your dad?"

"Yeah. He says the kitchen faucet's been running all day, and he wants me to come take a look at it. Why he needs that done right now at this hour instead of earlier, I have no idea. More than likely he's bored, lonely, or both."

Gone was the playful happy man I'd joked with, and in his place was a person who looked and sounded physically and emotionally exhausted. My heart wept a little for him, as I knew the strain of handling hard relationships with parents. "Is there anything I can do?"

He smiled tiredly. "No, sweetness, but thank you for the offer. I'll go by his place first and check on him, make sure he ate something tonight. I'll head up to the Lair after. It's closer to him than doublin' back and goin' home."

Again, there was a tiny bit of relief that he wouldn't be with Mallory later. Dodge had made a point more than once to tell me he was only giving her a place to stay for now and there was nothing between them. I wasn't sure how much I believed that on her part. I expected the woman had other intentions. Exes didn't just move back in unless they had ulterior motives, right?

Yeah, I was jealous. Somewhere along the way, I'd come to think of Dodge as mine. My guy. My biker. My man.

Stop it, Fauna. Dodge has enough shit to deal with, and you don't need to add any soap opera drama to the mix. If you can't be part of the solution, at least don't be part of the problem.

I cleared my throat. "Wait here for a minute." I hurried into the walk-in and pulled out two small go-box containers. "Take this to your dad. Just heat it up in the microwave. That's one task you don't have to deal with."

Dodge stared at the two white cardboard clamshells in his hands. "Thanks. Very kind, but you don't have to—"

"Pshhhht!" I copied Betsey's favorite noise and

flicked my fingers in perfect imitation. "You've been helping me ever since I got here. No reason not to give back a little. It's just chicken parm. Don't get too excited."

His eyes met mine, and he opened his mouth to say something, but his phone buzzed again. "He's gonna call me until I get over there. Thanks for this, Fauna. I owe you one."

I smiled. "Friends don't owe friends. Get going, and I'll see you soon."

<hr>

DODGE CRANKED THE SCREWDRIVER ONE LAST TIME. THE repair was a simple one. The rubber O-ring in the faucet handle needed to be replaced. Something his father had done in the past but now chose to call his son to come out and do. The excuse was the retaining screw was too tight. Boyer said he tried dozens of times but couldn't get the thing to budge.

Yeah, the screw was really tough to break free, but it wasn't so bad to need anything more than a bit of strength. It was possible his dad really didn't have the hands for it. Stuck or frozen parts were a daily challenge at the garage, and Dodge was used to that kind of torque. Luckily, he found the right-sized ring in his toolbox of random bits and was able to complete the repair.

He tested the handle several times, turning the water on and off. "There ya go, Pop. All done."

Boyer grunted something that sounded like "Thanks," then left the kitchen to plant his butt in the old recliner and click on the TV. The channel was one that showed old game show reruns from the seventies. Dodge shook his head. He couldn't imagine anything more boring, but then again, different people had different preferences. Some of his friends liked sports, and some liked movies.

He washed his hands in the newly fixed sink and wondered what Fauna watched during the tiny periods of downtime she had. Did she even have a TV? Probably some sort of Food Network type of show.

That reminded him.

"Hey, Pop, did you eat dinner already?"

"I'll microwave me some popcorn later" came the reply from the recliner. An episode of *The Hollywood Squares* started up, and Boyer's eyes were glued to the screen.

"My friend sent you something nice. Homemade chicken parm. I put it in the fridge earlier. You can heat that up instead of popcorn."

"Is that the restaurant friend you mentioned? Fauna?"

Dodge was pleased his dad remembered her name. "Yeah, that's her." He took a breath. "I like her a lot, Pop. She's good people."

"Mallory still living with you?"

Another breath. "Yeah."

Boyer kept silent a few seconds. Dodge waited for him to say something, then continued himself. "I was hoping she would move on by now, but she says she ain't got anywhere else but here." A frustrated sadness rose up in his chest with an unexpected dart of pain. "I have one woman in my house and another one in my heart. I'm not sure what to do about it, but I can't help the way I feel."

Canned laughter came from the TV. However, Boyer stayed quiet, and Dodge thought perhaps his dad had fallen asleep.

"Tearin' me apart, Pop. I held on to the hope for a long time that Mallory would someday be in my life, but I finally realized after the third or fourth time she left me that it would never come true. I gave up on ever having a future with someone, but then I met Fauna." He chuckled. "Crazy night when we got together. I thought I'd lost my chance, but she showed up here, in my town, workin' her ass off to make her big dream happen. I'm scared as hell to believe it, but I want this to be a sign that good things are comin' for me. That I finally found the person I've wanted and needed for so many years, and she'll stick with me."

Boyer still didn't say anything as Peter Marshall talked about the night's prizes. Ones given out years ago and were probably somewhere in a landfill by now.

Dodge gave a long sigh. Confessions like this weren't in Boyer Plott's wheelhouse, and seldom did the man have any advice on matters of the heart. Dodge didn't particularly expect the man to have some profound words or ancient wisdom on the subject of love and relationships, but once in a while, he wished his dad would open up.

Dodge picked up his tools and placed them in the box. "I'm beat. Gonna head up to the Lair and crash there tonight."

"Before you drive off, put that chicken whatever-it-is in the microwave for me. Your girl made it, so I might as well try it."

"*Your girl.*" Dodge's throat grew a small lump, and he had to swallow a few times. "Sure thing, Pop."

CHAPTER 15

I CLOSED MY EYES AND RUBBED THE LAST OF MY mascara from my lashes to my skin. My vision blurred from so many hours at the computer, setting up a website, plus all the social media sites. I was behind in advertising for the restaurant, but I finally had a launch date targeted, and now I had to build up excitement about it.

Dodge's habit developed into coming over to my place three or four nights a week after he got off work from the garage. Most weekends, he told me, he had to spend either at car shows or helping his dad. I thought that was really cool, but I was getting concerned about his well-being. Working nearly around the clock wasn't good for anyone. I made sure I fed him good food every time he came to see me and sent him leftovers for either him or his father.

Our conversations varied from food preferences to tourist seasons to weather patterns. We even debated some politics and religion, two of the most forbidden conversation topics. It was family we stayed away from completely. Without his help, I wouldn't be this close to seeing the restaurant open, just in time to catch the last of the summer season and open the fall with a real bang.

Hiring staff was also a priority. Few people had answered my ads, but there were some surprises. My saving grace came in that form exactly. A girl named Katie Grace who served in a local diner came in to interview, and I hired her on the spot. Her appearance was clean and professional, and her manner was composed and helpful. Just the kind of server I needed.

"Why are you leaving the diner?"

"Jimmy's gave me a raise but then cut my hours. Turns out I'm making less than I did before. I can't live on air and good luck wishes, so I thought I'd apply here."

Yup, I had all the work hours the girl wanted and then some.

My phone lit up and trilled next to my laptop. Macie's big kissy face profile pic appeared, and I smiled as I picked it up and answered. "What's up?"

"The sky and all the prettiest clouds money can buy."

I arched my back away from the bar chair, and my stiff spine shifted with several loud pops. "You're in a good mood."

"Yes I am, girlfriend, and you're about to be in one too. I quit."

"What?"

"I quit. I'm done with the Omni. Fee-nee-to. Terence and Juan came in the hotel bar while I was working and started up a little somethin'-somethin'. I am so not into those games. The manager said I had to be nice to them like I would any other patron. I'd rather be fucked by a bull than smile and serve them at my bar. Besides, I found me a sugar daddy, and he's already said if I decide to leave the resort, he'll set me up anywhere I want. It just so happens that I want to be in Bryson City for the rest of the summer and working for you."

Color me stunned. I needed someone like Macie to run the bar and charm the customers. He was excellent at his job, and I considered him a major asset, but… "Sweetheart, you know I can't afford to pay you what the Omni did."

His giggle sounded weird in my ear. "Dewey is real eager for us to get over there and get started. I told him about you and your restaurant, and he said he'd support me while I help you out."

"Support you?"

Another giggle. "Didn't I mention he's rich? His family has all sorts of businesses all over the state. He's got a hoity-toity vacation cabin over there and said it's ours rent free as long as we like." He gave a long princess sigh. "Our own little love nest built for two."

I couldn't help the laughter that burst from my mouth. "OMG, Mace. I've never heard you act so girly girl. You sound like a teenager with her first crush."

"My first crush was the high school football coach. I'll be at your place next week. You can meet Dewey later. He's got some business shit to deal with and will come see me next weekend. I'll be there tomorrow. Is that hunka-hunka burnin' love of yours still around?"

My brain immediately flashed to Dodge and his body as he lifted and moved booth components and tables. He'd worn only a thin tank that left nothing to my healthy imagination. All those yummy muscles worked together, smoothly moving under his skin. He caught me once looking backward at his beautiful ass and grinned at me. I was pretty sure I'd drooled.

"No hunkas here."

"Girl, you are one big disappointment. We're gonna be fixing that very soon."

Oh God, please no! "Macie, there's a lot happening right now, and I don't need you—"

A knock sounded on the door, and I shouted a quick "Come in." I flipped my head back to see the hunka-hunka walk in.

That's it. God has a real sense of humor.

"Honey, you need to get laid. Good and proper. That's what you need, and that's the man to do it."

"Bye, Mace."

"Oh shit! He just walked in, didn't he? Listen, gi—"

I hung up on my best friend before he added anything else to his plan. I'd dealt with Macie-in-love many times in the past. It was Macie-on-a-mission who scared the snot out of me.

"Hi, Dodge. You okay?"

He handed me my keys. "Car's done. Oil changed, filters, topped off the fluids. You should be good for a while."

I grinned. He'd offered last week to take care of my car maintenance for a steak dinner, and I'd made him a flambé steak Diane a few nights ago. Not really fully French but closely related. He didn't seem to care as he inhaled the filet and vegetables. God, how I loved to see someone enjoy my food!

"Thanks. You didn't have to bring it here."

"It's no big deal. I had the time, and the garage

isn't that far." His eyes roamed through the restaurant, approving of all the progress that had been made. "It's really taking shape, isn't it?"

"It is." I preened a little. I was getting closer and closer to my goal. So close that I could taste the succulent flavor. "I'm having a hard time believing this is really happening. I've dreamed of owning my own place for years, but it was always this abstract future idea. Now that it's here, I'm pinching myself constantly to make sure I'm awake."

I faced him directly in all my messy, sweaty glory. "I can't thank you enough for your help. This wouldn't be happening without you and Betsey and the club."

"I'm glad I got to be a small part of it." He turned, and those to-die-for eyes of his met mine directly. "I'm proud of you and for you, Fauna."

His words hit me square in the stomach, and I had to remember to breathe. My family held no support for me or my chosen profession, yet here was a man who said he was proud of me. Hell, his whole biker brotherhood threw down for me. To have that kind of loyalty was unfathomable. My eyes burned with potential tears, and my belly quivered. I wanted so badly to touch him that I could imagine the ghost of his body against me.

"You have no clue how much that means to me."

He read me so accurately that there had to be a magical connection between us. Some line that drew us together strong enough to be tangible. He stepped forward and wrapped his arms around me, enveloping me in a cocoon of warm maleness. It felt good. Real good.

We stood together for a long moment. I heard his breathing, sensed his heartbeat, and leaned into the balance of his weight on his feet as he stood over me. Solid. A firm foundation. It seemed the most natural step in the world for him to kiss me.

Or did I kiss him?

I didn't know who leaned in first, but our mouths met. Easily and sincerely.

It wasn't a kiss of hunger, nor was it tentative or awkward. His lips molded to mine as if testing for the right angle to fit. A glow started deep in my belly when his tongue darted out for a quick taste. Just that light touch was enough to make me open up to him for more. He took my invitation and raised one hand to the back of my head as he thoroughly explored my mouth. The kiss was a slow smoldering burn that fanned flames I thought I'd forgotten. I'd spent a night in bed with this man, making vague memories of promised passion, and I found myself craving another one. This time with me fully awake and taking part.

I wanted him inside me.

His body responded beautifully, and I could feel a hard outline against my stomach. Oh, how I ached to grind against him to relieve the broiling heat between my legs.

He pulled back suddenly. His face was rock-hard, and he held my shoulders in a fierce grip either to steady me or himself. Perhaps both of us. "I'm… I need to go."

"Dodge." My voice came out lower and huskier than normal. I cleared my throat and tried again. "Dodge." *Please stay. Kiss me again. Make love to me for real. Don't leave.*

I wanted to say more, I really did, but no words came out. What was it about this man that kept me from talking?

"Fauna, I can't. It's not right." A cup of sorrow, a pinch of desire, and a shit ton of regret tinged his tone.

Fuck me! Annoyance added itself to the mix in my gut. "Are you about to friend zone me, 'cause your body says otherwise."

"If things were different, I'd be taking you home with me now, but I'm not free to do that."

His expression showed pain, and my ire dissipated. Sure, I'd been betrayed many times in my life, by family, by boyfriends, by colleagues, so my first response of anger was well conditioned. However, this man hadn't shown me anything but support and concern, and it wasn't fair of me to judge him. Besides, he still had his ex living with him, and I was sure that had a part in his hesitancy. If Chase came crawling back to me, asking for another chance, I'd tell him to build a bridge and get over it, but Dodge was a different kind of man. Not once had he cut me down or said anything to me that made me question his motivations.

He gave a big sigh that sounded as if the world's problems rested on his broad shoulders. "I'm sorry. I shouldn't have kissed you. I hope you can forgive me."

I let it go. "No problem. Friend zoning is probably best for us, all things considered."

He jerked around and stiffly walked to the new elaborately carved wood door.

My memory dredged up the words I said to him so long ago the morning after we met. *"Let's just consider this to be a fond memory of the one who got away. Yeah?"* That phrase was valid then and needed to be valid now.

I hated it, but I had to accept the friend zone—at least for now. *If I can't be part of the solution, at least don't be part of the problem.*

"Dodge?" I called.

He paused with his hand on the latch.

"You've had my back ever since I met you. Please know I have yours too."

CHAPTER 16

Dodge pulled up to his apartment and shut off the bike's purring motor. The lights were on, and he stared at them for a long time. It had been a couple of days since he'd been anywhere but work or the Lair. To get to his place, he should have driven past the restaurant, perhaps stopped long enough to check on Fauna. Instead, he took a longer route that kept him away from her street. The memory of the taste and feel of Fauna's lips teased him, and he had trouble putting it away in a corner of his mind. He contemplated firing his bike back up and driving to the Lair for the night, but Mallory had texted him that afternoon and asked him to come home right after work.

Home. She used to say "come to the house," not "come home." He wished she'd use a different word.

"Hey, baby," she greeted as he walked in his door. "Dinner is almost ready."

When did he begin to think of himself as a stranger in his own place?

"I made your favorite. Spaghetti."

He spotted the Ragu jar on the counter. No, spaghetti wasn't his favorite, but it was easy to make. When they were kids, it was often the only meal they had available to them.

She set up the table and covered it with a plastic tablecloth he'd forgotten he owned. Two places were set, and a paper flower from the corner store sat in the middle stuck in an empty beer bottle.

Obviously, Mallory had put some effort behind this dinner. Her big smile reminded him of the first time she cooked spaghetti for them. She was nine, and he was eleven at the time. They'd been by themselves that evening and had to scrape a meal together with what they both had at their homes. He had boxed noodles; she had the sauce. The pot they made lasted several nights.

"Looks nice."

"Thanks. I got bread too." She set a plate of toasted sandwich slices on the table. "Do you want a beer or something else?"

"Beer is fine." He seated himself, then picked up a piece of the toast and slathered it with margarine.

Fauna would probably make her own sauce and bread from scratch. Hell, she might even make her own pasta instead of buying the store brand. Butter. She'd use real butter too.

Guilt landed in his gut so hard it stabbed like a knife. He was an asshole for comparing the two women. The scent of Pine-Sol told him Mallory had deep cleaned the apartment. Her clothes were no longer cheap skank but more modest and covered more skin. He thought it made her more appealing. She'd made him dinner and did her best to make it a nice one while he'd been dreaming of making love to another woman. After the one night a few weeks ago when he let Mallory sleep in the bed with him, he'd been living more at the Lair. Now guilt ate at him for not being around to encourage and see the changes she worked so hard to make.

Fuck, I should never have kissed Fauna.

He had no idea where this was going. His conscience wouldn't allow him to be with Fauna while Mallory lived with him, and he didn't want to sleep with Mallory even if it was platonic while his head was full of Fauna. Some men would gladly fuck both women, even suggest a threesome, and walk away when they were done.

He wasn't built that way.

"Dodge, are you okay?" Mallie's big blue eyes

appeared before him. Her bare face showed concern and a hint of tears. "Did I do something wrong?"

Her blonde hair was clean and brushed long in shining waves. When they were kids, he'd learned to French braid it for her. The strands would slip through his fingers as he wove the two thick plaits and tied each one off with rubber bands. Their world was closed to outsiders, and they only depended on each other. Looking at her now, he was reminded of that naive time. Since then, she'd played him over and over; he wasn't sure if this act was real or an attempt to keep him on her string. Still, there was food on the table and evidence that she was participating in the household business. If this was an innocent act, she was damn good at it. Maybe she had changed after all. Everyone had to grow up sometime, right?

"Nothing's wrong, Mallie. Thanks for doing all this for me."

She beamed happily at him, and the knife twisted a bit. He gave her his best facsimile of a return smile and picked up his fork.

CHAPTER 17

Tapping for the solid floor under my toes, I stepped off the ladder and walked over to the switch panel. I crossed my fingers as I scrunched up my face, concentrating hard, and flipped the tab up. The hanging lamps over the booths lit up with a soft bathing light.

"Thank you, YouTube," I said out loud to the silent room. I'd spent hours watching DIY videos on wiring, codes, safety specs, and procedures to the point that my brain hurt from the details. The time had paid off, though, as all I had to do was pass the inspection. It was scheduled for next week, and so far, I had everything running on time to make it work. The next round of lights would go over the tables, and the last set would be in the small bar area. I still hadn't gotten that area done, but I had a work-around if I needed it. The main goal was getting the restaurant part up and running. The kitchen was set up with the dishes, washed, stacked, and covered. All I needed now was a few more servers, a work-focused Macie, and to get the bar updated.

Two more weeks, I thought as I sat on the closest chair to rest my aching back and shoulders. *Two more weeks and I'll be in business.*

My energy waned early this evening, and I thought about stopping for the night and climbing the stairs to my current lodgings. The apartment over the restaurant wasn't particularly homey, and I was using it mainly because it was convenient. It had one of those cheap premade shower stalls that was so small, I had to stick my legs through the curtain to have room to shave them. My bed was nothing more than an air mattress on the floor, which probably didn't help my tight back muscles. The only closet was a rod I hung from the ceiling. It was rough accommodations, but every penny I saved now should help me get through those critical first three months after opening.

Macie visited once when he moved to town, but Dewey didn't come with him. Currently, they were at the coast on a brief vacation.

"You don't gotta pay me for now. I'll take my cut when you win that five-star rating. I already told you Dewey's

family has a place in Dillsboro. We can stay there for free. Dewey said he'll take care of expenses for us."

I didn't like that. It was only right to pay someone for their work, and I had every intention of doing so, but the reality was I needed someone with experience. Macie would be a big help in running front of house, even if that came from behind the bar.

My lower back twinged, telling me I needed to get in my so-so shower and use up the small tank of hot water. I stood and closed my eyes for my nightly prayer that a couple more experienced servers would answer the ad soon.

A loud knock interrupted my reverie.

"Hey, anyone here?"

I looked around to see a blonde woman standing just inside the door. The ragged edges of her blue jean cutoffs rode high on the sides of her skinny hips, and her short cowboy boots clomped as she walked over the shiny polished floor. "I heard y'all are hirin' waitresses."

She said the word like it was sour in her mouth. I remembered meeting this woman before. Mallory. She was the one who'd been hanging on Dodge's arm that night at the River's Edge. I'd only seen her the one time, but here she was in the flesh. And showing quite a bit of it.

"I prefer to call them servers."

"Whatever. I'm looking for a job, and I guess I can put plates on a table just as well as anyone else."

Little shards of pain radiated down my spine. I *really* needed that shower! "There's a little more to it than slinging plates around. I plan on having my servers practice the open-hand method."

Mallory sniffed. "What's that?"

I stood straight and mimicked the actions as I explained. "We serve from the left and clear from the right. Never cross the diner's body, nor touch the diner. Uniforms will be black pants, closed-toed flat shoes, and a white blouse. Clean, neat appearances. No perfume or scented lotions, as that would distract the diner."

Mallory looked confused. "All that to put out a cheeseburger?"

"McDonald's does cheeseburgers. I do cuisine."

Her eyes narrowed, and she opened her mouth to say something, but another interruption came through the door.

"Lord have mercy, just look at this place!" Betsey trilled as she walked in, her own boots clicking, with several square Tupperware containers piled high in her hands. "Never thought Miz Mae's diner would get this kind of makeover. Fantastic!" She whirled around to the woman behind her. "What do you think, Psalm?"

"I think I have some really nice artwork that will fill these walls perfectly and add to the color scheme." She reached out a slim hand to me. "Hi, I'm Psalm. I own the Soap-n-stuff craft store a few streets over."

I shook her hand, and the slight scent of lavender and vanilla drifted to my nose.

"Psalm is my daughter-in-law. Blue took the kids and the dogs to the park after closing, so we thought we'd come see how you're gettin' on and what we can do to help." Betsey's gaze shifted upward. "My goodness, them hanging lamps is real nice. Dodge help you get 'em in?"

"No, I did them myself." I hadn't seen Dodge in just over a week. He'd texted me a few times to say he had to work overtime at the garage on a project car, and his dad also needed him for roofing work on the weekend. We may be in the friend zone, but I still missed him. A lot.

Betsey turned back to face me with a big grin. "No kiddin'? That's fantastic. I love my boys, but sometimes it takes the ladies to get the job done." Her eyes moved to take in Mallory's presence and frosted over. Betsey nodded at her, but it was more like a queen begrudgingly acknowledging a less-than-stellar peasant. "Mallory."

"Hey, Betsey."

That exchange over, Betsey turned her attention back to me. "I hope you don't mind, but I asked Eva to come out for a bit to take a look at your bar. She's cut way back on her sewin' business and is itchin' to get her hands busy."

I frowned a little. "This Eva person. Does she know construction?"

Betsey gave me her *psshhht* noise, popped the *t* at the end, and flicked her bright talons at me, pink this time. The square plastic dishes nearly toppled. "Let me tell you what, darlin', that woman knows her way around a table saw. She used to work job sites all the time with her brothers. In fact, the bar at the River's Edge is her work."

I recalled the polished wood and clean lines I saw at Betsey's place. Yep, if Eva could make that magnificent piece, she would do fine with my little spot. "How much do you think she'd charge?"

"I'll be good with babysitting or some free meals for my husband and me in lieu of labor. Finding someone to watch my girls while Stud and I have some private time away is damn near impossible."

A fiery ginger-haired woman approached from the open door carrying a tool bag. If Stud was a Viking god, this woman was a Valkyrie. Colorful leggings covered her muscular thighs, and a long solid T-shirt draped over her tight, flat stomach. If she had more than one child, it didn't show. Either this woman spent some serious time at the gym or Betsey had not lied about her working construction.

She approached me with an open hand. "I'm Eva. Stud is my old man, and we have five stubborn alpha females under the age of ten. Now, where is your bar gonna go?"

Wow. Just wow. "I think that side in the back in sort of an arc shape. There's plumbing in that corner to tap into."

Her green eyes left mine, and she sauntered to the spot. "Good thinking. I can make this work. I'll draw up some ideas and let you know. You get the materials, and I'll take care of the labor. I can build most of the framing off-site and just do an installation. Won't take but a day or two at the most."

Alpha females, indeed!

"You got an application or something?" Mallory's voice broke through my reverie. Truthfully, I'd forgotten she was there.

"I have a general one upstairs. If you'll wait here for a minute, I'll go get it."

Betsey sniffed. "I'll follow you up. We made a whole mess of barbecue this afternoon, fixin's an' all. I figured I'd bring you some so's you won't have to cook."

Psalm let out a small giggle. "Of course it wasn't just an excuse to see the progress on the restaurant."

Betsey ignored her. "We had extra, and I'm bein' neighborly. The nosy part is separate."

I burst out laughing at the women who'd bombarded my life and insisted they become a part of it. "I don't have a kitchen up there, just a room and a pretend bathroom."

Betsey's eyes popped. "No kitchen? Are you coming down here to cook? What are you eating?"

I stopped laughing. "I suppose it's a little weird for a chef to be doing mostly microwave instant food, but I spend so much of my time working to get this place ready, I've been eating a lot of sandwiches and chips, or making a big pot of something for leftovers." I didn't tell her I'd been cooking for Dodge. I wanted those times with him to be private.

Psalm shook her head, and Eva swore a soft oath. "You've done it now. The kraken is released."

What?

"Oh hell no. I need to see this apartment." Betsey stomped to the back of the restaurant and piled the containers on the prep table. "Ain't none of my people gonna live poor when I got the means to make it better."

When did I become "her people"?

I barely caught up with her as she opened the

narrow door and climbed the steep steps to the apartment. One look at the air mattress on the floor was enough. Betsey spun around and ticked off her fingers. "No proper shower, a fake bed, and a mini fridge ain't an apartment."

At first, my reaction was mute anger. My mom had done this shit to me so many times in my life that I'd lost count. The constant barrage of criticisms and disdainful comments had conditioned me to be defensive at all times. Unfortunately, that also made it easy to be labeled as the angry Black female if I said anything or showed my irritation, so I chose my words carefully. "I don't—"

Betsey held up a regal hand. "Don't mistake me, darlin'. That's not a cut to you. You're workin' too damn hard to not have a real place and a real bed for your back. I seen you stretchin' it, and I done heard it crackin' when I walked in the door."

Her tone turned more motherly than I'd ever experienced, and my ire whooshed down the drain. "You need a long soak in a hot tub, a good meal, and a real bed for sleepin'. I cain't really tell you what to do, but I'm going to. Get your stuff together and come on up to the Lair. I got a whole guest suite that's private and empty right now. The boys'll be messin' around the big room, but you'll have some space and a nice firm mattress. None of this air shit.

Katrina's runnin' the bar up there tonight, and she'll make you one o' her world-class margaritas. Tomorrow, I'll help you find better furniture for up here. We got plenty stored up. No need for you to be campin' over the restaurant. Land sakes, I seen tents in better shape."

I grabbed one of the generic job applications I'd downloaded and printed. "I'm fine here, Betsey. Really."

"You may be fine, but I won't be. I won't sleep a wink knowin' you're livin' like this, especially when I can do somethin' bout it. Please, for my sake, come up to the Lair and relax a bit." Her eyes twinkled as she tempted me again. "Hot tub and a cold margarita? Don't tell me you're gonna turn that down."

My lips twisted ironically, and I raised both eyebrows. "Damn, Betsey. Does anyone ever tell you no and get away with it?"

She tossed her head and smiled. "Not very often. Brick thinks he's gettin' away with tossin' out my kale salads, but he hasn't figured out the veggie burgers yet."

CHAPTER 18

The Lair was calmer than he'd expected it to be. Dodge entered the open part of the clubhouse and noted the lounging bikers. Forge sat on a plush sofa with Donna perched on the arm above him. Rafter was next to him, and both men played a racing video game on the huge flat-screen. A couple of other men were shooting pool and drinking beer. Katrina sat behind the bar, but instead of mixing drinks, she had several books open. Dodge recalled someone mentioning she was going back to school for a bachelor's degree. Her pregnancy was showing quite a bit. Mute was over the moon with his second round of impending fatherhood.

Dodge stretched, and a bone popped in his back. Lately, he'd spent most of his free time either at Fauna's place or at the garage, working on the

Karmen Ghia after he completed his regular work-load. The reasons were twofold in that he loved working with the vintage restorations and he could avoid going home. Mallory had settled herself there and treated the place more and more like her own. She'd mentioned she was job hunting yet again, but in the meantime, she kept the apartment clean and cooked for him sometimes. He wondered if she thought they were getting back together because it certainly seemed that way. He saw her efforts, and even if he was working somewhere else, her texts told him she was home nightly instead of out finding the next party.

It wasn't all bad. The nights he came to the apart-ment, they talked about their days over whatever dinner she made and sometimes watched a Netflix movie. She would ask about his current projects at work and mention places she'd applied to or been turned down from.

The problem was he'd been down this route so many times, and even though he'd started thinking she'd changed, he didn't quite trust her yet. The blow job she gave him that first night hadn't been repeated, but that wasn't for her lack of trying. She'd backed off a lot, but the offer of sex was still on the table, and he knew beyond a shadow of doubt that if he traveled that road, he'd find major heartache at the end. So far he'd resisted, but twice now, she'd cajoled him into sleeping in the same bed, and like any man when confronted with a naked and willing female body, he was finding it hard to stay away.

Honestly, he missed the intimacy of being with someone on a deep level, and the idea of having that again was more temptation than physical sex. Easier and safer to make the extra effort to sleep in his room at the Lair.

His muscles pulled at the tight tendons, and he groaned. The work he'd done at his father's place hadn't done him any favors. Boyer needed a new roof, and rather than contract out for it, he'd pushed until Dodge gave in and helped him with it. Dodge had volunteered to pay for a company to do the work, but his father insisted on doing it himself. The last thing Dodge wanted was to get a call from the hospital saying his dad fell off his house and broke something. This past weekend, he'd worked nonstop to get the new shingles in place, and he was paying for it now.

Fauna did a lot of physical work herself as she prepared her restaurant for opening. A picture of her came to his mind, one where they'd worked side by side one afternoon. She was sweating profusely with straggles of curly black hair escaping the twist at the back of her head as she shifted another booth seat into place and anchored it to the floor with a hammer drill he'd brought over. Her body was so slight, and he wondered how she kept up with all the physical work her profession demanded, but she never shied away from it. Fuck, he admired her so damn much. Even with no makeup, puffing from exertion, messy as hell, he still wanted to kiss her. Again. But he was afraid if he did, he would never stop.

The guilt ate at him. The idea of one woman in his house and another one in his thoughts bothered him. A lot. Perhaps it shouldn't.

But it did.

Dodge waved at the other bikers and went to his room. His body hurt, and his mind was tired of thinking about his life. He needed to find an oasis soon. A break. Maybe a vacation?

He grunted and pulled an old pair of swimming trunks from his bureau. He would prefer spending time in the hot tub alone, but this time of night, there may still be people around. Betsey declared the pool and hot tub a no-nude zone after catching him skinny-dipping, and he wasn't about to disrespect the woman. He remembered at the last minute to grab a towel and then headed to the back door that led to the deck.

The pool water was smooth as glass and lay undisturbed in the fading day. Overhead, stars winked into existence as the light waned into dark. The bubbling noise told him someone else occupied the hot tub. His desire for solitude almost had him turn around to leave, but the pull of heated water soothing his aching back overrode that want. His steps were quiet as he walked barefoot to the raised pavilion that housed the hot tub, but he stopped when he saw the dark springy curls wound in a loose bun above the ties to a swimsuit top.

Fauna. Fauna was here.

Fuck.

His mouth dried up, and his body flashed on full alert. The heart in his chest revved from idling to a hundred miles an hour. He had to open his mouth to get enough air into his starving lungs. He stared and debated between running away before she noticed him and joining her in the steaming, bubbling water. His back wanted the relief. His body did, too, but a different kind. His brain stalled as the two desires battled themselves.

Helpless, he watched as Fauna realized his presence. She sat up and, in a slow-motion movie, turned her head elegantly to fix her eyes on his. The moment they locked gazes, something loosened in his chest. He was free-falling and couldn't stop himself.

Her face softened, and she smiled as if it was the most natural thing in the world to see him here. It had been days since he last saw her, yet she greeted him like no time had passed. "Hi, Dodge. You can join me if you want."

The husky tone of her voice hit him low. He should have apologized for disturbing her. He should have casually excused himself and left. He should have done anything else but get in that tub with her.

He lifted his leg over the edge. "Thanks." His body settled against the opposite side of the six-person tub, and he sighed as the heat seeped into his muscles. Yes, he could do this. Just soak for a little while, have a light conversation, and go to his room. Easy peasy.

Yeah, right.

"You look tired."

Her voice sent a thrill through his belly. He leaned his head back and ignored it. That and the shimmering image of her sitting across from him in what looked like a peach-colored bikini. "I am tired. It's been a heavy week at the garage. I'm booked out for three months on custom paint jobs, and I've had to pull double duty in the regular shop to keep up with the everyday stuff. Nice problem to have, I guess, but my back is not happy with it."

Her laugh sparked another wave of longing inside him. "I hear you. For years I ran around a kitchen, heaving full stock pots, chopping vegetables, stirring, and sautéing. I thought I was in good shape and had stamina to die for. Nope. I'm sore from lifting and hanging all those lamps today, and I'll probably be sorer tomorrow." Her nose scrunched up. "Is *sorer* a word?"

He huffed a small laugh. "I don't know. Maybe."

"Well, it is tonight."

Silence ensued for a few minutes. Dodge's body relaxed further into the water, and the tension melted in the heat. He let his arms float freely in the lightly churning water, and the hum of the tub soothed his nerves. He heard her give a sigh as she, too, let go. "You shouldn't be doing work like that by yourself, sweetness. I could have come to help you get that done."

"You said yourself you're working overtime at the garage. When exactly are you supposed to have time to come see me?"

"I'd make and take the time."

"What would Mallory say about that?"

A muscle in his neck cramped under sudden tension. "She doesn't get a say-so. Yeah, she's still at my place, but we're not together again."

"Is she aware? She came by the restaurant today looking for a job and only halfway filled out the application. I got the impression that she didn't like me much and only begrudgingly asked for a job because she needs one, not because she wants one. I wondered if it was because she thinks I'm competition or something."

He thought about that for a moment. "I've tried to be honest with her from the start. I don't understand it myself. I care about her and probably always will, but I don't love her. I can see her tryin' to get back with me, but I can't go back to being with her. At one time, I hoped we could work out a life together. But it doesn't matter anymore. In the end, she cheated on me. Left me. Over and over and over again."

"Love dies when it's not fed."

He raised his head in her direction at the statement, but all he saw was her silhouette under the pale moonlight. The cramp knotted harder, and he winced at the sudden pressure.

"I know that look. Here, let me help." She moved closer and faced him, leaning over to dig her strong fingers into the hard spot. It hurt like hell but relaxed as she worked it.

She sighed. "Chase and I got together at the culinary academy. We started out great—two friends who became lovers. We were going to take over the restaurant world and set it on its ear. I discovered his love had conditions, mainly *me* helping *him* succeed, not *me* helping *us* succeed. When I said I loved him, I loved him. When he said he loved me, it actually meant he needed me. It was like I was there to support him and make him look good, and when I stopped doing that, he turned on me. Not equal partners. Make sense?"

Dodge thought it did in a roundabout way. "I can see the difference. I'm sorry that happened to you."

She shrugged. "I'm over it. I just wished I hadn't wasted any time with a man who had no real feelings for me. At least I woke up and got out. If I'm going to have my dreams come true, it's up to me to make that happen. I've got more challenges than most people because of being Black and being a woman, but I'm also more determined."

Dodge leaned his head back to rest it on the hard edge and give her better access. Her hands felt so good on his skin that he was loath for her to move away from him. "I admire you, Fauna. You're a smart and beautiful woman with a great gift. I'm really sorry the world can't see that and appreciate you."

"Thank you for saying that."

He chuckled with his eyes closed. The burbling water flowed around him, and his mind drifted. "It's true."

If things were different….

Paintings of her rose in his mind combined with his art. Fauna as a warrior in a chariot pulled by lions

—no, lionesses. Flowing white dress. Not that. Gold ribbons, strategically draped over her body. Flames— gotta show the fire inside. Nah, dancing. Dancing on a beach. Not that either. Dancing naked under the stars.

The last picture that flashed behind his eyes had his body tensing up. Naked Fauna. Beautiful and captivating. Lying in a tangle of sheets, sleeping from exhaustion after coming hard. Even though he'd deleted it from his phone, the memory was still vivid in his brain. He would paint her with softer colors and blend the effect. *My Queen* would be the title.

Her hands still worked his shoulder, and he groaned as blood rushed to harden his groin. "Fauna, you need to stop."

"Why?"

Had her voice grown huskier? Did touching him affect her the way it did him? "I'm having a hard enough time staying away from you as it is. Just knowing we're under the same roof tonight is bad enough, but having you right here, right now? It's fucking torture. You make me want things I have no right to want."

"Who says you can't have what you want?" Her fingers dug through a painful knot, forcing its release.

All the pressures came at him in one swoop: his

apartment, the garage, Mallory, his father, overtime, the club's new troubles, the restaurant, his feelings for Fauna. It was too much, and the dam broke as he gave in.

Her body was light and buoyant as he moved her onto his lap. Her legs straddled his, bringing her core closer to his. Only two layers of clothes impeded any intimate contact. Both of his hands ended up in her springy hair, and her mouth met his in a rush of hunger.

His dick swelled painfully against the chafing swim trunks, and he wished like hell he hadn't bothered to put them on. Her slick skin glided over his, and he groaned as her tongue licked at his lips. One tension flowed from his body as another took its place. Her arms came around his neck as he plundered her mouth. He hooked a finger at the top of her bikini and pulled the triangle of cloth down to reveal her nipple. She broke off the kiss, gasping when he plucked at the tight tip, which gave him the opportunity to draw it into his mouth and circle the rough areola with his tongue.

"Dodge," she breathed huskily. "We started off ass backward that night in the hotel, but that doesn't mean there's nothing between us. Don't you think it's time we dispense with the friends-only thing and do something about this?"

God, how he wanted to. It had been a long time.

So why not?

Why was he hesitating? Some sense of chivalry? Honor? What was stopping him from consummating this draw between him and Fauna? He was an expert at mixing and blending colors into beauty. What reason existed for him not to be with the woman he wanted so fucking badly?

He let go of her breast and bared the other one. She cried out again as his lips covered her other nipple. "Please, Dodge!"

His dick ached with need. It would be simple. All he had to do was raise his hips a little to pull the annoying trunks down and free himself. Then he'd move the crotch of her bikini over and finally be inside her. He imagined they would both explode in seconds.

He slid his hand down between her legs and under the thin layer of cloth. She was soaking wet even in the bubbling water. He slowly pushed a finger into her hot channel, and she moaned into his mouth. "Yesssss."

His thumb snuck between the fleshy lips and stroked over the hard nub of her clit. He noted that she had let her pubic hair grow back and wondered if she would ask him to shave it once more. After he did, he would go down on her again and again until he exhausted her from coming so many times. Then he would spread her thighs wide and…

He lifted up and tugged at his trunks.

"Yo, Dodge, you out here? We got us a case of Jessop's 'shine. The one with cherries in it."

The burst of voices from the back deck worked better than a dousing of cold water. Fauna yelped and awkwardly fell off his lap, going under the waterline and coming up sputtering. She jerked her swimsuit back in place and moved to her original spot across from Dodge just as four people appeared around the corner. Rafter and Forge approached the hot tub with a large glass jar of ruby liquid and a sleeve of red plastic cups. Two women were with them, ones Dodge had seen around the club but didn't know. He wasn't sure which irritated him more, the shit-eating grins of his club brothers or the girls' drunk giggles.

"You naked in there, brother?" Rafter finally spotted Fauna, and his face changed to an *oh shit* expression. "Looks like you two were having a conversation. Fuck, should we leave?"

Dodge gritted his teeth and swore Fauna blushed as she scrambled out of the hot tub and grabbed her towel.

"Nope. I'm done for the night. Y'all have a good

time." She paused in her flight. "Oh you've got to be kidding! I just said *y'all*."

The others laughed at her joke, but Dodge kept quiet and did his best not to squirm with discomfort. His trunks were still in place, but his pulsing erection would be on full display if he moved.

Part of him was angry as hell at the interruption.

Another part was grateful.

He watched as Fauna retreated without a backward glance. The quartet of new people laughed and flirted as they stripped and climbed in the bubbling tub. Bare breasts and asses splashed into the water with a burst of giggles.

Rafter poured a round of the 'shine and added a couple of the potent cherries. "Here, brother. This shit is the best."

Dodge took the plastic cup and downed the contents in one go. The fire burned to his belly, and his dick finally softened. He caught one of the round fruits in his back teeth and chomped down, filling his mouth with sweet cherry and biting alcohol.

If the prospects and their women hadn't come along, he would be inside Fauna right now, making her come.

Afterward, she would have hated him.

He cursed under his breath as he rose from the water. "It's been a long week. I'm hitting the sack.

Have fun, but don't let Betsey catch y'all naked out here."

One of the girls laughed loudly, making her wet breasts bounce above the waterline. "He said 'y'all' too!"

Forge said something in response, but Dodge didn't hear it. He ignored the sounds from the hot tub as he toweled off and quickly left. The main room of the lodge was empty, the TV off, and the players retired for the night. Dodge's gaze drew to the staircase that led to the upper floors. Brick and Betsey's private quarters were up there along with the guest suite where he guessed Fauna lay. He was tempted, so fucking tempted, to climb those steps and see if she would let him in. The cherry taste in his mouth was nothing compared to hers.

He waited for several long minutes before going to his own room. Hopefully, he would find some sleep this night.

CHAPTER 19

"Oh snap! This is perfect for the front area so people can sit while they wait."

"You're so right. What's the price tag say?"

I groaned as Macie and Betsey moved as one unit to examine a wood bench. Both of them decided to accompany me on a discovery shopping trip to the local antiques mall. I wanted to add some finishing touches to the bistro's decor with locally made pieces and a few extra odds and ends.

Psalm brought me some gorgeous paintings and other wall art that blended together. She'd also offered some really nice pottery from a reclusive artist who lived somewhere deep in the mountains, saying, "I've never met the man, but his face jugs are very well known throughout the state."

I'd take any support I could get from name recognition, even if that name was just "potter on the mountain."

I'd spent several nights at the Lair while Betsey insisted on outfitting my small apartment. She had Rafter and Forge move a spare queen bed and dresser she had in storage to my place, plus some lamps and a small love seat.

"Cain't do nothing 'bout a better kitchen, but at least you got a decent place to sleep for now. You can always come to the Lair anytime you want to," she'd said.

I'd teared up a little at the warm invitation. It seemed when Betsey claimed someone, she did it all the way with no expectations of payment or future favors. She'd accepted me into her group completely, and I grew more and more comfortable in that fold. Tambre told me to come to her salon anytime and she'd take care of me. Molly wanted to take me shopping for new clothes whenever we got a day off. Eva had finished the bar and took me to hang with her at the River's Edge once when Stud's band was playing.

"The girls are spending the weekend with their uncle and aunt in Asheville, so I'm taking advantage of having a night off to see my husband play," Eva explained. "My brother and his wife only have three kids left at home now. Their oldest decided to do college after all. Beverly is an amazing mom. Connor is so damn lucky to have moved in next to her."

Yes, I had friends now. Female friends with no agenda whatsoever. This was a level of acceptance I'd never had before, and it blew me away.

The one fly in the ointment came in the form of a tall linebacker-built blond man who occupied my thoughts constantly.

Dodge was into me, or at least I thought so. The scene in the hot tub percolated in my mind for the past week and drove me crazy. Part of me was angry as hell at him for not following through. Another part respected him for not pushing me into a potentially embarrassing situation after I threw myself at him. I bounced back and forth between the two emotions with a healthy dose of anxiety for flavor.

I stifled a groan as my two decorators chatted and shopped like old friends. Hormones. That had to be why I nearly jumped the man. It had been a long time, after all. He liked me, I liked him, and those pesky little enzymes ignited in a surprise flambé.

Should I ignore it? Acknowledge it? Try again? Or stop it?

There was no running away, as we were around and supported by the same people. What would happen if we suddenly broke off this friendship or relationship or… fuck me sideways, I had no idea what to call this thing between us.

"Oooh, look at that plant stand!" Betsey and Macie were examining a wood spiral holder that could house a number of smaller plant pots. My bartender grinned at me. "You can put this up front and grow fresh herbs in it for the kitchen!"

I wanted to be irritated, but the piece was cute and matched the bench. "I can't grow enough oregano in one of those little pots to season more than one or two dishes."

Betsey flicked her nails at me. "People will see the fresh stuff and think what they want. It's a good marketing visual."

She had a point. I left them to wander around and found myself at a back wall looking at row after row of framed prints of vintage motorcycles. Not really part of my restaurant theme, but they were still pretty cool. Some of the models looked like they were the first ones ever made, as in really primitive, but one short squat one painted in green and white caught my eye.

"A 1936 Harley Davidson El Knucklehead. One of the rarest vintage bikes out there." Betsey joined me as I stared at the picture. "Dodge had the opportunity to do a restoration paint job on one for a collector some years ago. I remember the guy wanted some sort of *Star Trek* theme with the Starship Enterprise on the side. Dodge convinced him to keep it classic like this one. He really likes you."

I bit my lip as my heart leapt up to dance. "It's… complicated."

Betsey put her arm around my shoulders, and my throat pulsed with the need to close. "I get it looks that way, but it ain't. Dodge has some scars and baggage in his life, and from what you've told me, you got some mess too. He has a big sense of obligation to take care of the people in his life, and some of them have taken advantage of that. His daddy is one. Mallory is another. Breaks my heart to see any of my boys hurtin'. Dodge hasn't shown much interest in any woman for years. That is until you came along."

"I don't know what I'm doing, and I don't know where I stand," I confessed. *Why do I have the need to talk to this woman?* "There are challenges between us, and I haven't a clue what they are or how to handle them."

She squeezed my shoulder in a side hug. "One step at a time is always best. Dodge will figure it out, and you will too. All I can say is be patient with him. If y'all can see your way through, I can tell you now, you won't find a more loyal and trustworthy man than him. That boy needs someone to love him unconditionally, and he's never had that before he came to the Dragon Runners. All my boys have special places in my heart, but it's not the same thing as having a partner. I hope it works out. If it don't, I'm gonna tell you right now, the club will have your back no matter what."

My mouth opened, and I shoved my foot right inside. "Does the club still have Mallory's back?"

Betsey's grip slackened a bit, but she didn't let go. "Now that part *is* complicated. I'll admit, Brick and me don't like her much. She's been in and out of Dodge's life so many times over the years, playing games and using him, and it drives me crazy. The club is about brotherhood and family. Every single one of my boys would lay down their bikes before hurtin' a Dragon Runner's woman. That's sayin' somethin' 'cause you already know how they feel 'bout their bikes. Mallory betrayed that code over and over again, and I watched it take little pieces of my boy away. I don't think she ever figured out what she was doing to him. She's got her own problems consuming her, and I realize that, but it don't take away the pain she gave."

She dropped her arm and moved to pull the picture off the wall. "Brick has a thing about club women, to always protect them no matter what. Mallory was one of us at one time. If she's in trouble, it's deep in his nature to take care of her as we can, but it's really hard to take someone back when they've hurt someone you love."

I turned my head and noticed her eyes were wet. Betsey also felt it deep. A pang hit my heart, not for Dodge but for me. Biological or not, this was what a mother's love looked like, and it was huge. "I'm so glad Dodge has you in his life."

She handed me the picture. "Funny, I'm thinkin' the same about you. Remember I came by one night when you and Dodge were pickin' at each other while you was fixin' up the restaurant? First time I heard him laugh in years."

"Oh! My! Gawd!" Macie exclaimed. "Betsey, my dearest, you have *got* to see these shelves! They are to *die* for!"

"I'll be right over."

I wondered if their volume would get us thrown out as I stroked a finger over the print. Dodge would love to have this, and I wanted to give it to him.

Was that crossing a line? We were friends now. Perhaps more, but there was a shit ton of secrets he carried. Would there ever come a time when he would be free enough to be with me? Did he want to?

Yeah, I was sure he would be with me if he had the chance.

CHAPTER 20

Dodge carefully taped off the car's hood for the next color. This was a tedious, complicated piece that had taken him hours to design and customize. The multicolored iridescent spider was the centerpiece with its reflective white-and-silver web covering the rest of the black car. It was the intricate detail that took a long time to get right. The client was paying big bucks for the work, and Dodge was doing his best to make sure he delivered.

It was hard as his mind was full of other ideas.

"That's gonna look damn good at night. I bet it scares the shit out of someone."

Weatherman stepped into the spray booth and closed the door behind him. He kept a good distance away from the car, as dust and other particles were forbidden here. The booth's exhaust was off until

Dodge finished the taping; the noise level was deafening when both the venting system and the air compressor were turned on. "I hope so. I'm charging him enough." He checked the angle of a leg and swore as he had to peel off the blocking tape and reposition it. Again. "You just get into town?"

Weatherman slipped his hands into his jean pockets and leaned back against the coated cement wall. "About a half hour ago. No one is up at the Lair, so I thought I'd stop here before heading to the house."

"How's your mom?"

"She's taking her first chemo in the morning."

"Good luck to her and to you, brother."

Weatherman dipped his head in acknowledgment. The younger man could have been Dodge's sibling. Both had sandy blond hair and blue eyes, but where Dodge was built like a brick house, Weatherman had the body of a runner, slim and toned. "She's got a long way to go, but the doctors say the surgery went well. As soon as I finish my contract, I'll move back permanently. Until then I'll keep commuting."

"Sorry you have to give up your dream job."

Weatherman shrugged. "It's my mom. I can always get another anchor position. The station said I could come back when I want. If I want."

Dodge tapped the tape in place and rechecked. After prospecting during a gap year between high school and college, Weatherman had earned his degree at UNC-Asheville in environmental sciences. Just after graduation, his good looks and articulate voice got him snapped up by the local news station over in Knoxville, Tennessee, as one of their meteorologists. The guy oozed charisma and charm, and everyone agreed he was on his way to the big leagues. Then his mom got sick, and him being the only child, he moved closer. Originally, he and his mom lived just outside Asheville, but Weatherman's mentor and club sponsor was Table, who resided in Bryson City. The older biker helped get his protégé and mother moved to a small cottage close to the Lair so the two of them had the support of the entire club. They did as much for Natalie Turner as possible, but it was Bryce Turner, aka Weatherman, who ultimately took care of her.

"I hope it works out," Dodge said as he straightened. "I'm almost ready to spray. You wanna stick around for a bit, or you got other stuff to do?"

"I gotta go get a haircut, and then I'll head over to the house. Moving sucks."

Dodge chuckled. "I hear you. Take care, and I'll see you at the Lair later."

The paint was already mixed. Four air sprayers of

different sizes sat on a rack near the compressor. After zipping up the paint suit, Dodge slipped on the vapor mask and safety goggles. Last, he put on the ear cans, then started up the loud machines.

As he put on the first layer, his phone buzzed in his pocket. Once he started painting, he couldn't stop, so he ignored it. Then it started again.

And again.

And again.

Dodge cursed for not taking the annoying device out of his jeans and leaving it in the office while he was in the booth. Distractions might cause him to ruin a job and have to start over. Many hours of prep had to happen before the first coat of paint got applied. On detailed jobs like this, he had to be extra careful, as any mistakes would put him days behind schedule. Maybe even weeks.

The phone kept recycling its ring repeatedly until Dodge finished the blended coatings for this round. His hand popped down on the kill switch harder than necessary as he jerked down the zipper to his suit and pulled out the phone.

Twelve unanswered calls. *Twelve.* All from Mallory.

Dodge took a deep paint-fume-tinted breath and called her back.

"It's about fuckin' time!" she snapped.

He bit his lip. If anyone asked him, he would swear on a stack of Bibles that they weren't back together, but Mallory was acting more and more as if they were. "I was in the booth. You know I can't answer the phone when I'm working."

"I need a ride to work. My car's not startin'."

"I'll call one of the boys to come get you."

Her tone turned from crisp and irritated to contrite and whiny in an instant. "No, Dodge, please. They hate me and won't help. Everyone is so mad at me all the time. You're the only man in the world I can depend on. Please help me."

Dodge swore in his head. Why did he let her get under his skin? "Mallie, I really can't leave what I'm doing. I'm already behind and getting further as I'm talking. Can you take an Uber?"

"Get in a car with a stranger? Please don't make me do that."

Dodge's resolve crumbled. His options were to stand here talking and wasting time or take care of Mallory's problem and work more overtime to get this job done. "Okay. Give me ten minutes and I'll be there."

"Thank you, baby."

He peeled down the spray suit to his knees when the next call came in.

"I need you to come over. Got a tree needs cuttin'," Boyer greeted.

Dodge wanted to throw the phone. "Pop, I'm really behind, and Mallory just called for a ride to work. Can it wait?"

"It's a two-person job."

Dodge reached for his reserves of patience, but the writing was already on the wall. "Is there anyone else you can call?"

A big sigh came through the phone, laying it on thick. "It'd be nice if my son would help me out from time to time."

Dodge closed his eyes. If it were possible, he'd get on his bike and ride away. Pull over somewhere on the Tail and disappear from the world. "I gotta go take Mallory to work, and then I'll come out. Anything I need to bring? Second chainsaw?"

"I only got one."

Before Dodge could say another word, his father hung up.

He pinched the bridge of his nose as his brain rearranged the rest of his day and the next few to accommodate all the work he had pending. Christ, a single hour away from everyone and everything would be delicious. Almost as good as the meal Fauna had cooked for him some nights ago when he went over to her place to help her plumb the new bar Eva built.

Mallory heard about it and got jealous.

"You're all the time up in her business or over at the Lair. You never come home no more. You'd rather be with that b—"

"Don't go there, Mallory. Say the word and you'll find yourself in your car tonight."

Fauna. Her opening night was a few days away. The same weekend he was booked for a car show in Winston-Salem. The Dragon Runners were planning on being there in support, but he wouldn't be. How the fuck did he forget the most important event in her life?

Simple. She didn't beat him over the head with reminders. She was the one person who didn't need rescuing.

She was also the one person he wished needed him to rescue her. The foiled night in the hot tub still haunted his thoughts. Every time he remembered that heavy "Yesss" as he—

His phone trilled with another text, and he gritted his teeth. Mallory.

> Mallory: Are you coming!?!?
> Hurry up!

He glanced at the half-finished spider in the spray

booth and added a trip to Starbucks for a large coffee with extra shots to his to-do list. He hoped this tree job his father wanted wouldn't take too long and he could get back to work before his body stopped functioning.

CHAPTER 21

Opening night. I spent the morning with my gut twisted into knots the size of boulders and my head pulsing like it wanted to explode.

Macie was my anchor. Whatever God was sitting in the universe pulling strings did right by me in sending my favorite bartender here. He had the experience I needed, plus great charisma with the customers. It would be tough for him to run front of house and tend bar, but he was capable of both. I hired two high school busboys who would take turns washing dishes and clearing tables. There were four servers, which would push me hard, but I was used to timing for big crowds. No full sous-chef, so I'd done all my prep work earlier and readied my kitchen for the influx of people. I did have a college kid who was studying culinary arts at the local college; he would assist me with plating appetizers and desserts.

The weakest link was Mallory, but she was dressed appropriately, and her hair was neatly pulled back in a clip. She might have looked the part, but her attitude had been lacking throughout the training. Her condescension showed more than once, and she got downright hostile at times. If I didn't need every warm body I could get my hands on, I never would have hired her.

My menu was a blend of French and American dishes: coq au vin, beef bourguignon, and salmon en papillote next to a grilled rib eye steak, Cajun blackened chicken breast, and fried catfish. The stews and soup starters were bubbling away on the warming stove. Salad veggies were chopped and ready to be made up. Everything I could get accomplished ahead of time to make dinner service flow had been done.

My head pounded with anticipation, my stomach was tied in one big Gordian tangle, and the urge to vomit lurked in the back of my throat.

I was ready.

Macie gave the pep talk to everyone in the dining room while I stood alone in my kitchen. *Mine.* The word bounced in my skull like a pinball. This was my restaurant. My kitchen. My business. It could all go wrong in a heartbeat, or it could be the culmination of a lifetime dream.

I closed my eyes and breathed in the scents. Savory, sweet, salty, spicy, all blended into one big mass that closed off my trachea and choked me.

What the fuck was I thinking? Opening an upscale bistro in a small mountain town? I was going to fail. No one would come eat my food. I'd be bankrupt in a month and a laughingstock. Other chefs and restaurateurs would point at me and shake their heads at my audacity to think I, Fauna Somers, would ever be successful at this.

I should just shut it down now and take my losses before—

"Go time, sugar pie. There's a whole mess of people at the door waiting to come in."

Macie popped his head through the double door as the busboys and my assistant sauntered in. Through the opening, I could hear the sounds of people entering the restaurant and the scrape of chairs as they sat down at the blue-and-white-striped covered tables.

Another huge breath cleared my thoughts, and I stood tall. "All right then, babycakes. Let's do this."

Time passed. Fast or slow, it didn't matter as my focus was solely on my food. Getting it cooked, plated, and served. I had my assistant bark out orders as they came in and call for pickup when plates were ready. I didn't know who was in my dining room, only what they wanted to eat. My hands flew over the pans: season and broil, flip, time the steaks, check the fish, and order up. Plate after plate left my hands into those of the servers.

I had no time to think of anything else. Tables turned. More people. More food.

Did I make enough soupe à l'oignon, or would it run out midservice? Was that last steak too fatty to serve? Were people ordering more salmon or catfish, and how should I adjust menu items?

The last ticket of the night was called, and my body relaxed for the first time. If there were any problems on the floor, Macie said he would go over them with me after service was complete. My shoulders burned, and my legs shook as if I'd run three marathons back-to-back. The busboys were washing up the last of the dishes before I finally sat down at the bar.

"Here, girlfriend. You earned this." Macie placed a shot of Tennessee's finest in front of me along with a glass of ice water. "Reviews are already coming in. Looks like you've scored a hit."

I ignored the shot for a moment and gulped the water. "What are they saying?"

He scrolled and turned his phone to me, and I skimmed over random phrases.

Excellent food!

Mountain treasure found here.

Good atmosphere. We'll be back.

Terrible napkins.

I blinked at that one. "Terrible napkins? What the hell does that mean?"

Macie rolled his eyes. "I knew you'd pick up on that one instead of focusing on the good ones. There was one lady here, a Burna someone-or-other, who complained the napkins were too small." He sniffed and popped a raspberry through his lips. "It would take a whole tablecloth to cover that thigh spread of hers. She insisted on sitting at a booth and complained when she had trouble sliding in and out of it." Macie held up a hand and ticked off his fingers. "She also didn't like the decor 'cause it wasn't like it used to be, didn't like the colors, didn't like pictures, didn't like the silverware style, didn't like the lamps—"

"Did she like anything?" I laughed. This wasn't the first time I'd heard about or dealt with unhappy diners. There were some people in the world who would never be pleased no matter how hard you worked at it.

"She must've liked her steak. Bitch practically

licked the plate. She had her granddaughter with her. Poor little mouse kept quiet and ducked her head when her grandmama started in on something. Dewey said it was like watching a turtle fold in on itself."

"Dewey was here? Why didn't you bring him back so I could meet him?"

"He had to get back to Asheville for some kind of business something. He said to tell you he really likes the place and looks forward to coming back soon." Macie sighed his dream-girl sigh. "I swear I love that man more every day. The things he can do with his—"

"Stop!" I held up my hand, palm out. "TMI. I don't need to hear a blow-by-blow account of your sex life, my friend."

Macie grinned. "You said *bllooooooow*."

"I'm done with you."

The other staff came to the bar for a rundown of the night. Weariness showed on every face, but they were all happy with the accomplishments of the evening.

I looked around. "Where's Mallory?"

Katie Grace's smile fell a bit. "She left just after service. Took her tips and walked out. I cleaned up her station for her."

I frowned at the foreboding sense that she

wouldn't be back. No big loss, as she had done the absolute minimum, but still, it was a body I needed to replace ASAP.

"I have a cousin looking for work. I can see if she wants to apply here," Katie's sweet voice piped up. Apparently, she'd come to the same conclusion I did.

"That would be fantastic. Now, let's hear about tonight and what we can do to make it better for our customers and the staff."

I smiled as my people bounced around ideas and made suggestions. Yes, we were all exhausted and ready to drop, but the excitement of success glowed in every face.

My only disappointment was that Dodge hadn't been able to come. I understood why. Work was work, and he had an obligation to it. Still, seeing him in my place, sharing in this important night, would have been the cherry on top of the cheesecake.

"People ordered more of the catfish than the salmon," Katie Grace noted.

I nodded and refocused on the task at hand. "Got it. What other menu items should we change?"

CHAPTER 22

Dodge came off the highway and slowed as he approached the city. Four days he'd been gone to a car show. The lumbering box truck held a 1986 Ford Thunderbird that had once run in the local drag races; it still had the decal numbers painted on the sides. It had been a good trip. Excellent for the show and even better for the business.

He paused as he moved through the downtown streets. At this hour, most shops were closed, but there were a few still open. This had been Fauna's opening weekend, and he'd received multiple texts about it from several club members. Tonight, Sunday, was the third night, and she planned on being closed tomorrow.

On impulse, he drove down the street and saw the restaurant lights still on. Katie Grace and several other people exited. The big smiles across their faces told him his brothers hadn't lied and the restaurant was successful. He waited to see if Mallory came out.

She didn't.

A light rain made pattering noises on the truck's roof as he parked at the side of the street, confident of little to no traffic at this time of night. This was the same vehicle he'd used to transport all the restaurant stuff from Asheville, and the width took up more than its fair share of road space. He tested the front door and found it still open. Macie and Fauna were going over some papers at the bar and didn't hear him at first. She looked tired as hell but radiant. A tightly wrapped bun of heavy hair sat at the back of her neck. The chef's smock she wore had multiple stains on the front, and any makeup she might have had on earlier had been sweated off. Still, an aura of beauty surrounded her, and he found himself pulled forward.

She raised her eyes to his, and he nearly tripped. Even disheveled, she was breathtaking.

"Hey, Fauna."

"Hey, Dodge. I didn't expect to see you tonight."

"I didn't expect to come home tonight, but here I am."

Both of them fell silent. It was Macie who broke it.

"Well, kiddie-winkies, I'm off. I gotta get my

beauty sleep before Dewey comes home." He waggled his fingers. "See you Tuesday, my darlings."

Dodge nodded to the smiling man as he exited.

"How was your trip?" Fauna asked with a tired smile.

He put his hands in his jeans pocket. "It was good. I found some parts I needed for the Goat and found some other sweet deals. Got a couple more clients for custom work. We'll see if they follow through."

She laughed. "That's always the risk, isn't it? The follow-through."

He barked his own laugh. "Yeah. Most of the time, I get ghosted, but then there's a few who bring their work to me."

The rain picked up, and he glanced through the front window. It was coming down steady and soaking. This was a good thing, as it had been a dry summer and they needed it badly.

"Are you hungry?"

Yes, but not for food. "I could eat."

"Come on in the kitchen."

She pulled out her personal stash of beef bourguignon leftovers and reheated them as he seated himself at the kitchen prep table. The succulent smell filled the air. She placed a bowl of the rich stew in front of him along with some pieces of baguette. He made himself eat slowly, not shovel it in his mouth as fast as possible. "This is great, Fauna. Thanks."

"No problem. I'm glad to cook for you anytime." She set a glass of red wine in front of him. Wine wasn't his preferred drink, but he lifted it to his lips for a sip. The flavors blended perfectly, and he nodded his appreciation. "You're really good at this."

"At what?"

"Food, wine, the whole thing." He scraped the last bit from the bowl with a crust of the bread and popped it in his mouth. "Damn, that was the best meal I've had in days." He let out a soft belch and finished the wine.

"I have some chocolate raspberry petit fours. Care for a sweet?"

Yes, but not the ones you offer on a plate. "Sounds nice."

She poured more wine for both of them and pulled out several of the bite-size treats. "I'm not a real French pastry chef, but I can make these pretty easily."

Sugary snacks had never been his thing, but the small squares were perfect. Not too sweet and just the right balance of tart berry. He ate three of them, and she had two.

The silence of the room tightened. Tension

ramped up in his gut. For what reason, he wasn't sure, but something was in the air.

Maybe it was the sound of the rain coming down in sheets outside.

Maybe it was the superb food.

Maybe it was his fatigue from the weekend or from fighting his attraction.

Maybe it was a combination of everything.

He didn't know who made the first move. All he knew was one second she was next to him, and the next she was in his arms, her mouth beneath his. The taste of wine and chocolate touched his tongue, and he reveled in it as she opened to him.

Want filled his mind and body. The kind of want he'd given up on ever having in his life. The woman in his arms filled every sense in his body, and the desire to claim her sang through his vein. It wasn't just sex—he could get that anywhere should he care to. It was the whole package. Conversation, support, tenderness, humor, kindness, all the things that made up a partner in life, that wrapped up into one neat little word.

Love.

Fucking hell, I love this woman! He loved every part of her and wanted nothing more than to shout to the world that she was his and they were together.

And it was the very thing he couldn't have.

He pulled away, fiercely taming the beast inside him. "I gotta go." His voice sounded rough in his own ears. Gritty, hard, unyielding. It had to be that way, at least for now. He hoped she wouldn't hate him.

"You can stay." Her breathy words raked over his ears. He heard the desire in them, and memories of her gasps and moans as she came under his mouth assailed his will. The thought of her taste nearly sent him to his knees.

"I can't."

"Why not?"

"Please, Fauna, I can't."

"Oh, for fuck's sake!" she let loose. "We've been circling each other for months. You feel it. I feel it. We're both adults, and we want each other. What's the problem?" She threw her hands up in frustration, then pinned him with a withering look. "Don't tell me it's because I'm—"

He didn't let her finish the question. "No, goddammit! You know me better than that."

"Then what the hell is wrong?" Her volume increased with exasperation.

He couldn't blame her for getting angry. It was a shitty thing to do, leading her on, flirting with her, touching her the way he did so long ago, only to drop a bomb like this on her.

But she needed to know. She deserved to know why he blew hot and cold at the same time.

"I'm still married."

***

DODGE DROPPED OFF THE TRUCK AT THE GARAGE AND unloaded his bike to drive home. He was almost swaying on his feet with fatigue.

He pulled up to his apartment and cut the engine. His thoughts were still on the woman he left back at the Smoky Mountain Bistro. Fauna had shut down after his confession. He saw all the emotions drain from her face in an instant as the words left his mouth. She didn't show rage as he'd expected. She didn't cry. She didn't rant. She didn't indicate pain. She just shut down and turned away, leaving him alone in the middle of the empty restaurant.

It would have been better if she gave some sort of reaction. Anything would have been better than the cold that pierced him when she left. Hell, he wished she'd punched him repeatedly with her fists and loudly cursed him.

"Fuck," he swore and leaned his head forward to rest on his hands draped over the steering wheel.

He had the divorce papers in his desk at work. Already signed by him, but he'd never filed them. He should have finished this business a long time ago but never got around to it. God, how he wished he had. Divorce in North Carolina was possible without consent, but the year-long waiting period reset every time Mallory came back in his life. Perhaps he might have pushed it, but even after all this time, he still had a soft spot for the little girl he grew up with, and his sense of responsibility for her had never really gone away. He'd wondered for the longest time if they would ever become the couple and family he hoped for. But those dreams had died so many times that he should have been immune to her by now.

He thought he was destined for a life of being single in a toxic marriage. That was until he met a woman at a hotel bar and spent the night with her. Fauna made him think of the future and what it would be like to wake up next to someone. To have a partner, a real one, who stood by you and with you through thick and thin. Brick had that with Betsey, Mute with Kat, Stud with Eva, Blue with Psalm, and Table with Lori. He'd wanted that with Mallory so badly, but over time and multiple disappointments, that desire had disintegrated into no more than wishful thinking.

And it killed him to think that he had a chance with Fauna and epically blew it before ever really getting started.

He sighed. He was tired as fuck. Physically, emotionally, and spiritually. Maybe he would go over and see Fauna tomorrow. Talk to her and lay everything out. If she would let him in the door. First, he had to talk to Mallory and settle the shit between them once and for all.

He dragged his feet as he climbed the steps and entered the dark apartment. The first thing that struck him was the silence. No lights. No movement. Nothing.

An empty hollowness started at the base of his spine and crackled as it moved up and over his shoulders. He didn't have to check the bedroom to be certain as the familiar feeling of betrayal engulfed him.

Mallory was gone again.

CHAPTER 23

"You're gonna dig a hole in that thing if you keep going at it like that."

Macie was right. I looked at the marks I'd made on the grill top with my frantic scrubbing and realized I'd committed the cardinal sin of scratching off most of the seasoning. *Fuck me sideways!*

"I'm still married."

Those words had been ringing in my head for days. After he dropped that bit of wisdom on me, I had the rare experience of being speechless. Nothing, not even a cold shower, could make me drop from a fever-pitched four-fifty to subarctic zero in a nanosecond.

"I'm still married."

How was that possible? What good did it do him to stay married to a woman who obviously had no commitment to him? Did he still love her? Why would he subject himself to that shit?

Love dies when it doesn't get fed.

I dropped the scrubber and shook my head to clear it. "Fuck."

"Something's been biting your ass for a couple days now. You wanna lay it on me, girlfriend?"

Macie and I had spent many nights over the years drinking throughout our conversations on men, jobs, world slights, and any subject that took our interest. More like drunken bitch sessions about anything and everything, but this news about Dodge, I needed to keep it to myself for a while. "Nothing bad. I just have a lot on my mind. How's the POS working out?"

Macie's pointed look told me my subject switch didn't fool him, but he let it go. "The point of sale is working just fine. Mallory is the only one who has a problem with it. I'm pretty sure I can get her up-to-date—that is, if she ever shows up for work again."

Mallory had been absent for several days, and under normal circumstances, I'd have already fired her lazy ass. Since she was—*ugh!*—married to the man I wanted to be with, I was afraid that would open me up to more problems. Possibly the legal kind, but that would be hard to prove. Then again, the entire staff could back me up as to her job performance. The one and only night she worked for me, only the absolute minimum was done, and throughout the service, I heard her complaining about demanding customers.

"The old bitch at my table wants a new fork 'cause she dropped hers on the floor. It ain't been on the ground that long."

"Asshole over there's mad about the onions in his salad. Yeah, he said he didn't want no onions, but cain't he just pick 'em off like everyone else?"

"Hm. That damn cow in a dress don't need no dessert."

I'd also observed her sneaking phone calls during the busy shift. From acidic grapefruit juice to sugary Southern sweet tea, she turned it on and off in the span of a heartbeat.

"I'm done at ten. Want me to bring you some food, baby?"

"I miss you so much."

"I'm coming home soon, honey."

I figured out it wasn't Dodge she was talking to. He was at a car show that weekend, not to mention her vibe was wrong. Dodge was being manipulated. Anyone could see that, but was it my place to say something about it? Especially given my feelings toward the man?

It had been days since I'd seen him, but he stayed

at the forefront of my mind. Over and over again I replayed each encounter we'd had. The nights he spent helping me in the restaurant. My car. The hot tub. The hotel on the morning I found myself in bed with him. Sometimes we simmered and sometimes we boiled, but we never quite reached temperature. I knew why now, and it was like getting blanched with an ice-water bath.

"I'm still married."

Macie flung a hand at me. "If you're gonna sulk about whatever it is all day, at least go sulk at the salon. You're looking like a Pomeranian having a bad day."

He was right. My hair needed cutting. Badly. I could no longer ignore the puffed-out frizzy mess on top of my head. Hair care had been a big deal for most of my life, but I'd let it slide the past few months because of time. The tiebacks and headbands no longer worked, and I had no choice left but to visit a salon. Tambre had offered to help me if I visited her place, and I didn't know anyone else around here, so therefore, I took her up on it.

The door to the salon dinged when I opened it. A TV was showing some morning talk show with the sound muted and captions scrolling across the bottom. The buzz of hair dryers mixed with the country music playing over the speakers and a light pungent scent of perming solutions tinged the air.

A couple of ladies with wet hair sat in chairs. A girl with pink tips worked on one, and a pretty blonde worked on another. All of them were White. I wanted to groan out loud. Driving all the way to Asheville would take more time than I had to give, but did the hairdressers here have a clue about Black hair? I didn't want to make a big deal of it, but I also didn't want to end up looking like a blown-out poodle either.

I was about to turn around and leave when Tambre came out the back. Her soft eyes lit up when she saw me in the waiting area. "Fauna! I'm so glad to see you. Are you here for a trim?"

I hesitated. Tambre had been nice and supportive ever since I met the woman. She and her husband—"old man" I'd heard her say once—were regulars at the bistro and came every Thursday night. Katie Grace usually served them and remarked that they were generous tippers. Tambre never struck me as a negative or prejudicial person. Perhaps her own heritage made it easier for me to voice my concerns. I took a big breath, then leaned in to whisper, "Um… can you handle my type of hair?"

Tambre smiled, and I let out a held breath. "I understand, and yes, we can. I'll work on you personally if that would put your mind at ease. When did you shampoo last?"

In no time, I was sitting back in the shampoo room of her salon, my head leaned back in a sink and her hands running through the tangled mess on my head.

"Your ends are really dry. I think it's time for a deep conditioning treatment. It'll take an extra thirty minutes, but I'm sure you'll like the results." Her fingers dug into my scalp. "This is really nice, though. The curly texture is fine, but you have a lot of hair."

"I have a Black mom and a White dad," I said out loud. This surprised me, as I didn't share that with strangers, but something about these Dragon Runner matrons seemed to emote calmness. The slow, deliberate movement of her washing my hair, the warm water over my head, the massaging of her fingers as they worked in the fragrant shampoo, all of it made me feel at ease, and I opened up. "My dad is the CEO at one of the largest banks headquartered in Charlotte. My mom does the charity thing. She's on the boards for this and that—save the whales, save the books, save whatever the going trend is. My brother is a doctor. A surgeon, actually. One who gets his picture taken for all the medical magazines. I was supposed to be another doctor or lawyer, but I chose a different path. So far they haven't forgiven me for it."

"You feed people."

"There's nothing that special about me."

She worked the sprayer, placing a hand over my forehead to shield my eyes. "There's something special about feeding hungry people. I'm going to use the personal blend I make for my hair. It's got jojoba oil, argan oil, and grapeseed oil in it. Not too heavy for finer hair shafts, and it'll help with breakage. I have it for sale here, and Psalm carries it at her store."

I gave a short laugh. "My mom used to tug and curse at my hair when she tried to style me as a kid. I hated when she used a straightener on me. She took me to a fancy salon once, but they messed it up worse. Knots the size of golf balls because the products weren't meant for my hair type. They had to cut them out, and I looked like a sheared sheep for months."

The wide teeth of the comb glided effortlessly through my curls. Whatever she had in that conditioner, I was going to buy a case of it. She kept talking as she worked her magic into my hair.

"I grew up on the reservation. I had one brother and three sisters, all of us living together in a three-bedroom trailer. My parents didn't believe in owning a TV or video games, so that left a lot of time to fill after chores. My sisters and I would spend hours playing with each other's hair. I learned to braid. Box, micro, twist, sometimes I did ombre and yarn weaves. We were the most stylish girls in school. Instead of cutting yours, I can do a few rows on top to keep everything away from your face and leave the rest to flow behind. Your curls are so nice—they just needed a little love. Want to try?"

Tears suddenly hit my eyes. "I never had braids growing up. My mom didn't allow them."

Tambre hummed again. "Sounds like you had a tough upbringing."

"Some people wouldn't agree. I had money. Lots of it."

"Money doesn't mean happy. My family was dirt poor, and for the most part, we were happy." Her deft fingers pulled a few strands from my forehead. "We did have our problems sometimes. The word *dysfunctional* gets thrown around, but if you ask me, the perfect family doesn't exist. Everyone has challenges, some more than others, but I think it's how we face them and who we face them with that counts. Take my Taz for example."

I felt gentle tugs at my scalp as she worked. No pain, which surprised me a little.

"My father didn't want me dating a White man. I

met Taz when I attended school for the first time outside the rez. I had to get my cosmetology license, and the only place that had it was the tech college over in Sylva. Classic story of my car breaking down on the highway one night after class. Cell phones were around, but not everyone had them back then. I was alone and scared and had no way of calling anyone."

She pulled another section and started braiding that. "Long story short, this group of bikers pulled up. I was terrified. We'd heard stories about how White men treated rez women all our lives. I was sure I was going to be raped or worse. Then Taz spoke to me."

My curiosity burned at the woman's story. "What did he say?"

"'Ride with me and I'll always protect you.' I've never forgotten that moment, when he reached out a hand to me and I got on the back of his bike. That was it. We've been together ever since."

I didn't know what to say. It seemed she was imparting some life lesson to me, but I wasn't able to see it. Yet.

Another section of hair lifted into her nimble fingers. "My father hated it. He yelled at me for weeks, declaring how terrible a daughter I was for not obeying him. He wanted me to stop seeing Taz, but I was stubborn. I'd met my lifemate, and nothing was going to make me give him up. Some people called us being together a sin, but I discovered something a long time ago."

I held my breath as a weight settled in my chest.

"Love is never a sin. It's messy, it's complicated, it's frustrating as hell sometimes, and it will make you want to scream, but it's never a sin."

Tears filled my eyes. *Fuck me, why am I crying?*

"There we go. Have a look. What do you think?"

She spun the chair around to let me see what she'd done. Across and back from my forehead were six rows of tight, neat braids about two inches long, leading to a defined mass of soft curls. They were perfectly formed and hung in a curtain that framed my face beautifully. "These are so good. I never felt any pain."

"You shouldn't. Pain means damage. There are ways of braiding without pulling roots." Tambre fluffed the curls, and they bounced softy. "Do you have any idea how many women would love to have hair like yours?"

That startled me. My hair had been the bane of my existence for so long, the thought never occurred to me that people wanted hair like mine. "Not many, I'm sure, but thank you."

She fluffed again. "You'd be wrong. Thick,

gorgeous curls, soft natural shine, a variety of lengths and versatility. Plenty of women out there want this kind of hair on their heads." A soft chuckle reached my ears. "They pay me big bucks every day to help them get it."

Her eyes shone into mine from the mirror's reflection. "Don't let small-minded people keep you from having all the happiness this life has to offer. That includes family."

Damn, Tambre had some serious insight. A burning started in my throat. "Thank you."

"No problem. It's on the house today, and if I'm not around, Opal over there can handle you. She's just moved here from Minnesota and is an excellent colorist. If I trust her with my hair, I can trust her with yours."

I got up from the chair and brushed at my eyes. *Why did I suddenly tear up? Time for my period, I guess.*

She walked me to the door and smiled. "Dodge is a good man. He takes care of everyone around him. I hope he finds someone to take care of him."

CHAPTER 24

Zelda Bask stomped out of the bar and shot the door a drunken finger. *Fuck them and the fuckin' horse they rode in on!* Her fierce thought stayed in her mind because she couldn't connect the words to her mouth. Every night after her shift at the Sheetz gas station, she came to Reaver's bar to drink and get as wasted as possible. *Why the fuck not? I make my own living, pay my own bills. Who the fuck are them people to cut me off and tell me to go home? Ain't nuthin' else to do in this bumfuck town. 'Sides, I ain't drunk that much yet.*

"Iz ma' munee, ya' mudder fuggerz!" she yelled at the parking lot and almost fell to the ground.

Oops. Maybe they were right, and she'd had too much this time. Maybe she did have more than the two vodka tonics she remembered? That meant vomiting. *Ugh!* She hated that part.

She staggered again and lost her footing completely. Before her sodden brain could react a pair of hands caught her.

"Hello, pretty lady. Slow down now. It's dangerous out here for a woman alone."

Her head lolled back, but her eyes could not focus on the man in front of her. "Imb dot drung."

He chuckled. "I didn't say you were, but you *have* been drinking tonight, haven't you?"

Zelda smacked her lips together. She had a salty, dry taste to her mouth. "Yeah. Wann-uther wun. Fuggerz kickgged me oud."

He tsked. "I'm sorry those assholes treated you badly. If you really want another drink, I'll take you someplace else."

"Fuggersh."

"My car is over there."

Her eyes rolled funny when she turned them in the direction he pointed. His legs started walking toward the car that blurred in her fading vision. Hers all but dragged as she tried to make them work.

"I'll take care of you, pretty lady."

"Mrrrghrrsh" was her last word before the world faded to oblivion.

CHAPTER 25

The client came to pick up the spider car and was thrilled with the work. He made promises to send others to Dodge for custom jobs.

Dodge thanked him graciously but hoped there would be some time off between jobs. The extensive paint work took days, and other work in the garage suffered. Table was a tattoo artist and sometimes helped with drawing a design and shading, but most of the work came from Dodge.

He walked into the break room and pulled out a Dr Pepper from the fridge. A plastic container with Brick's name on it caught his eye. Another kale salad that Betsey packed for him. This one would find its way into the trash can just like all the others. Dodge suspected the woman knew her efforts to get Brick to eat healthier were going to waste, but that didn't stop her from trying. Maybe it was stubbornness on both their parts, or maybe it was genuine care. Brick and Betsey teased and poked at each other, but no one could deny the devotion between the two of them. It was a tangible thing, visible by anyone who watched closely. At the Lair, when Betsey brought a beer to Brick, she would pause and rub his shoulders. If Betsey called the shop for Brick to pick up something on the way home, he never argued but asked if there was anything else she needed. Brick made tough calls for the club, sometimes ones that only he knew the reasons for. Betsey might or might not agree, but she never undermined him or contradicted him in public. Her place on the back of his bike was cemented in stone and sealed forever. Dodge knew how rare that kind of love was and wished like hell he had a chance at it.

"Take that shit over to Christina and Andrew Thompson. They have all them rabbits they raise."

Brick's surly voice made Dodge grin, but he kept his mouth shut. "Sure thing, boss man."

The older man humphed and plopped down in one of the plastic deck chairs kept in the break room. "Wish that girl of yours opened for lunch. That steak she did up for me was some of the best I've ever had."

Dodge's heart jumped at the casual phrase. He

wanted like hell for Fauna to be his girl, but he expected that chance was gone. "She's been thinking about the lunch thing. Says she doesn't have a lot of people right now and is trying to build the business to support more hours."

Another humph. "I heard Mallory done picked up and left again."

Dodge fought not to grind his teeth together. He thought grieving was supposed to happen at the end of a relationship, but if it did, he'd already blown past denial and moved on to the anger. "Yeah."

Brick grunted once more. An "I told you so" would never pass from his lips, but Dodge sensed it anyway.

Yes, Mallory was gone. She sent one text to say she needed to get away for a while. *Get away from what?* Dodge had pondered. *The job? The apartment? Life?*

Me?

After finding her gone, he'd thrown himself into work, trying to erase the rage he felt at being abandoned again. She'd taken all the cash he had in the apartment and a couple of items to pawn somewhere. Thankfully, he'd kept his bank and credit cards in his wallet where she couldn't get them, else she probably would have cleaned him out completely.

She'd done it before.

Brick didn't need to vocalize anything, as Dodge was kicking his own ass for being fooled.

Again.

No. This was the last time. For years he'd waited in the hope that his first love would turn around and be the woman to stand by his side. That wish had been dashed so many times, he'd turned into an emotional shell. Yes, he made the motions, but when it came to real feelings, he was a wasteland. Mallory took advantage of him and his love for her and turned it into a circus with him as its clown.

Dirt washes off, he thought. *I don't have to live like this. I'm through being a convenient punching bag for someone who can't appreciate me and what I bring to the table. I'm through being an ATM. I'm through being a workhorse on call. I'm through with being taken advantage of.*

I.

Am.

Done!

There was almost an audible click as his spine elongated and he felt himself growing tall. It was as if several hundred pounds of dead weight slid from his shoulders and the world opened and became lighter. The sense of freedom was intoxicating. He could do this. He could love someone and be loved back, working as equals together to build something special in this life. It was time to stop living half-truths and commit to himself so he could commit to someone else.

Fauna. Would she still have him? He needed to talk to her.

Shit, I hope it's not too late!

"Brick, you gotta read this."

Bruiser galumphed his bulk into the small area and placed his ever-present iPad on the table. A breaking news bulletin scrolled across the top of the screen. "Weatherman got a heads-up from his buddies at the news station. They found her this morning."

Local woman's body discovered near campground. Investigations underway.

"It's Zelda. Remember, I dated her for a bit some years ago. Mean as a snake and drank like a fish. We broke up because of it. Says here there's some mysterious circumstances 'bout her death. Not only that, the bartenders at Reaver's said she was drunk as hell from two vodka tonics." Bruiser's huffing breath filled the room as the man panted from exertion. "That woman could drink six or seven vodka tonics chased by a dozen shooters and it not faze her. Hell, I watched her down a bottle of Jack Daniel's like it was bottled water. Ain't no way two drinks would make a dent in her. Somethin's fishy, but I cain't get no one at the sheriff's office to tell me what's goin' on."

Brick focused on the electronic device. "Reaver's is over in Whittier. That ain't far." He picked up his phone and dialed. "Blue? Bet you know why I'm callin'." His face grew tighter and tighter as his son spoke. "Yeah, I know you cain't tell me everythin'. I respect that, but I'd appreciate you to give me somethin'."

Brick listened a moment and then swore. "All right. Thank you. Bring yourself, Psalm, and the kids up to the Lair this weekend. Your mama wants to see you."

He swiped the phone closed and turned to the two other men in the room. "Church tonight. Make it seven o'clock," he said in a quiet voice.

Dodge's nerves jumped to hyperalert. Brick could be loud. He could shout the rafters down in irritation. He could command a room with his booming voice. He could stop all conversation with a bark that was as bad as or worse than his bite. But when Brick got quiet, he got dangerous. That was the time when heads would roll. Literally.

Bruiser inhaled audibly. "Brick, just so you know, I didn't love her or nothin'. She weren't never my old lady. We just hung out a few times, you know?"

Brick looked up at the big man and asked, "Did that woman come under my roof?"

Bruiser nodded. "Couple of times is all."

"You think it matters to me if she was there one time or one hundred times?"

Bruiser went silent, then said, "I'll send out a group text."

Brick turned his attention to Dodge. "Find Mallory."

CHAPTER 26

*D*AMN *COFFEE MAKER IS TAKING ITS SWEET TIME THIS morning*, I thought as dark brown liquid sustenance dripped slowly into the carafe. My norm these days was pretty much running on fumes and sheer stubbornness. Customers packed my restaurant every night this week. Tables turned several times, and the people kept coming right up until closing. The intensity of running with a skeleton crew was getting harder to maintain. I'd hired two more servers since Mallory left and still had trouble keeping up. I had to get another full-time chef and soon.

The machine gurgled the last few drops and hissed to let me know it was done with its morning duties. I sat at my little apartment table and sipped a cup of the heavy Sumatra brew. The flavor rested on my tongue, dark, earthy, and slightly bitter. Just the kick I needed this morning.

Last night went longer than I'd expected. Macie asked to leave right after service to spend time with his boyfriend.

I finally met the elusive Dewey, Macie's latest love interest. He didn't look like a rich man; off-the-rack jeans, plain button-down shirt, and box-store loafers—nothing made him stand out. The waves in his sandy hair looked neat and styled but not one of those three-hundred-dollar cuts. His eyes were a nondescript blue, and he didn't seem to want to be in the limelight.

That was hard to do in Macie's orbit, as my friend had the kind of charisma that attracted anyone and everyone. Macie was a good-looking, vibrant man, and people flocked to his outgoing nature. My perfect front of house guy and barman. I was sure that much of the repeat business I'd had came from his exceptional management and people skills.

A frown tickled my face as I finished my first cup of coffee and poured my second. Dewey and Macie. Macie and Dewey. "Opposites attract," as the saying went, but I just couldn't see them together.

Whatever. I had paperwork to complete and a trip to the bank to make before heading out for the markets. Fresh produce was essential, and in this foodie habitat, I had plenty to choose from. So far, my menu was a hit, but I wanted to change it up and add weekly specials based on seasonal items. Darnell Farms was a mecca of vegetables and fruits, and I loaded up whenever I went to their place.

I mentally sketched out a recipe for a Lyonnaise-style potato medley. The itty-bitty ones that were pretty much bite-size. Red-skinned, Yukon gold, and purple for a nice color palette, seasoned with rosemary, olive oil, and sea salt, roasted first in butter and then baked with caramelized onions. Little parsley sprinkle on top for another color layer.

I bet Dodge would eat it up.

Shit, why did I have to think of him?

Probably because he still hadn't come to my restaurant since his big confession. How did I feel about it? I really didn't know.

"Love is never a sin."

The other Dragon Runners had been to my place several times since opening night. Betsey and Brick were weekend regulars and brought an entourage with them every time they came. I was catching what was essentially the tail end of the tourist season, but from what everyone told me, there would be a second wave as people came to ride the train and see the fall colors.

Hmmm. Fall. Pumpkin spice everything. Perhaps I should think about a winter squash medley.

My phone trilled on the counter, and I picked it up without tagging the number first.

"Have you been reading your online reviews?"

My throat closed, and I choked on my coffee. I hadn't heard from my mom or anyone in my family in the months since I'd moved here, so her voice was a surprise. "Guh. Hi, Mother. What was that?"

"Your reviews. Haven't you been checking them?"

I coughed and cleared my throat as best as I could. "Not lately. There's so much to do and—"

"You have a three-star rating."

My gut plummeted. I skimmed a few of the reviews, but so far every one of them had rated the Smoky Mountain Bistro as five stars. Excellent food, exceptional service, outstanding atmosphere—all the buzz phrases that meant success. "What site was it on? Was there more than one?"

"It doesn't matter what site. What matters is the content. Yes, it was only one, but that's not the point. This diner was unhappy and left you a bad review. You need to fix it."

My head pounded with fatigue and barely held temper. "I can't fix it if I don't know the problem. I'll try to find it soon."

"See that you do."

The coarse dismissal in her tone had my heart racing and heat flushing over my tight chest. I'd worked my ass off for months, lived rough, been putting in twelve or more hours a day, seven days a week, and the first thing she did was point out a single bad review.

"Don't let small-minded people keep you from having all the happiness this life has to offer."

"Mom?"

I heard the heavy exhale on the other end of the line telling me I was disturbing her schedule. "Yes, Fauna, what is it now?"

"Did you read the five-star comments or only the three-star one?"

This time the noise she made was a sharp intake. "What do you mean?"

My stomach flipped over and threatened to bring up the coffee sloshing around inside. I seldom confronted my mother on anything, most of the time because it wasn't worth the fallout. However, this was my dream she was sticking pins in. "Have you been to my restaurant?"

"Don't be absurd. You know very well I haven't."

"Have you ever tasted my dishes?"

"I've eaten your cooking in the past."

"Saturday morning pancakes when I was nine

doesn't count. I'm talking about my signature recipes at the culinary school or at the Omni."

"I never got the chance. They fired you."

"I've been a professional chef for almost six years. In that time, have you ever been at my table?"

Another heavy sigh. I pictured her sitting on the edge of the plush sofa in her pristine living room, her hair beautifully coiffed in place, clothes in the latest styles, and makeup perfect. "Fauna, this interrogation is ridiculous, and I don't have time to play games with you."

"What right do you have to judge me?"

The phone got so quiet that I thought the call might have dropped. I continued on anyway. "You've never set foot in my place or eaten my food. I have people in this town who've supported me from the moment I started my restaurant. They've helped me with furnishings, staff, finding contractors —all the things I needed to get this place up and running. Betsey opened her home to me and got my apartment livable. Dodge took a day off from his own job to help me move everything and spent more than one night getting it set up. Eva built my bar for not much more than materials cost. My opening night, they all showed up to eat and enjoy my cooking. It was a massively good night for me."

"I do not know who these people are."

I started crying. Big, fat, honking tears rolled down my cheeks, and my sinuses plugged up, making my voice sound funny. "That's the point, Mom. You've never called me to congratulate me. You've never set foot in my place, not even on the most important night of my life. You've never eaten my food, yet you think it's okay for you to call and announce that I have a single three-star review as if that's a crime and then tell me I need to fix it."

"Fauna—"

"I get more love from the Dragon Runners than I do from the people I share DNA with. They are so proud of me and my restaurant. They have included me in their family, no questions, no qualifiers. Nothing I have to do to earn my place. I just have it. No, you don't know them, and if you did, you'd look down your nose at them."

I swiped my soaked face with my hand. Gross, but no one was around to see me fall apart. "I'm done. So done with this bullshit. I've worked fucking hard to get where I am, and I'm not going to stop doing what I love. You can either accept it or reject it. I don't care anymore what you think."

I hung up before she said anything else. Pain thumped in tandem with my heartbeat. I put my head down over my folded arms and bawled. I wasn't expecting this emotional confrontation with my mom today, but it was long overdue. I tried, but I didn't remember a single instance when she'd said "Good job" or "I'm so proud of you" to me. And when was the last time I spoke to my dad or my brother? Christmas nearly a year ago? I didn't go to his birthday party and wasn't missed.

It hurt. It hurt bad. I'd been through some pain in the past—breaking up with boyfriends, being passed over for jobs or promotions, getting judged by the color of my skin or texture of my hair—but this pain was new. My family, the people who were supposed to love me and be there for me through thick and thin, had abandoned me. If I was being honest about, they'd done it a long time ago. It felt like my heart was running through a grater at high speed, and I could do nothing but let the process finish.

I didn't know how much time passed, but the crying jag finally abated, and I sniffled. No doubt my eyes and face had swelled and puffed out.

I blew my nose and gave myself a lecture. "Stop feeling sorry for yourself, Fauna. You have two good hands, a refined palette, and a strong nose. Let's get it in gear and get to work."

It wasn't helping.

My phone trilled. I didn't want to pick it up to check; if my mom was calling me back, the last thing

I needed was to hear her blast me for hanging up on her. Instead, Dodge's name came up.

"Hey, I need to talk to you about something. I'm outside right now. Would you… can I come in?"

Fuck me, I don't want him to see me like this. "Um… yeah, sure. Hold on." *Dammit! Why did I say that? If I could kick my own ass, I would.*

"You sound funny. Are you okay?"

I lifted the edge of my shirt to wipe the mess off my face as I moved to unlock the door. "Yeah, I'm fine. I just… stubbed my big toe, and it hurt."

He didn't buy it. Dodge took one look at me, and his mouth dropped into a huge frown. "What happened?"

I thought I'd cried myself out. I was wrong. More tears trickled down my cheeks. "My mother… three stars… I… shit, I *hate* crying!"

"I'm not real sure how you feel about me right now, but I'd like to hug you. Come here, sweetness."

He folded me into his arms, and I burrowed into his warmth and wrapped myself around his strong back. There was a solidness to him that called to me. A sense of security that he wore on those broad shoulders as easily as his Dragon Runners cut. He smelled good. Light and spicy, and all man. Did I care about him and Mallory? Not at the moment.

"I'm gonna get snot all over you," my muffled voice said against his chest.

His chuckle rumbled under my ear. "I spend most of my days covered in sweat, brake grease, and paint streaks. Dirt washes off. A little snot won't hurt me."

I let it go and took the offered comfort, absorbing it like a dry sponge. I'd never realized how much I needed this. A connection with someone who genuinely cared about me with no other ulterior motive. With Dodge, I didn't have to work at it. I didn't need to be five stars no matter what. I didn't have to always have perfect hair and makeup. He had no expectations from me, just accepted me as I am. Warts, snot, and all.

He stroked his big hands up and down my back, and I couldn't help it. Right or wrong, future or no future, good idea or bad one, I let go.

And fell.

Did he feel the same about me, or was this just his habit of rescuing people?

Did he still want me?

Did it matter that he was still married?

No. No it didn't. By all indications his marriage was only on paper. There was no real connection between him and Mallory. He told me he cared about her but didn't love her and hadn't in a long time.

Why he'd never fully divorced her, I didn't know, but I expected he would tell me when he was ready.

I'd wait a lifetime if it meant having this man as a partner.

That soothing touch rested at the small of my back. "When do you have to start your day? Got any time you can take off this morning?"

"I can take about an hour."

"Come ride with me for a bit. My bike is out front, and it's gonna be a good day for it. I'll take you up on the Tail, yeah?"

My stomach fluttered. A ride with Dodge on the back of his bike. Yes, I would so do that.

I cleaned myself up but didn't bother with makeup. In no time at all, I wore that same heavy helmet and was sitting behind Dodge on his motorcycle. The familiarity of holding and leaning on him struck me as we pulled away and he drove through town. Once we hit the highway, I heard his voice in my ear from the speaker in the helmet.

"Hold on, baby. I'm going to open her up a bit. Stay with me and follow my lead, okay?"

The next twenty minutes were the most exhilarating I'd had in a long time. He tore up the hilly, twisting road, the bike roaring as he switched gears and leaned into the tight curves. Inertia pulled at me, and I moved with him.

The early morning fog swirled around us as we drove along. We were the only two people in the world, just us and nature. Contentment washed over me. I could get used to this. From the moment I met Dodge, even under those weird circumstances, he'd been nothing but kind and caring toward me. What I wouldn't give for this ride to last forever.

He pulled off the main road onto something that resembled a dirt path and slowed down. Tree branches made a canopy over our heads as he moved deeper into the forest. "I want to show you something," his tinny voice sounded in my ear.

"Okay." I hoped he heard me.

I expected the path to open to some magical clearing with a bubbling creek or pond. Nope. It came to a pile of rocks. That's it. A pile of rocks.

"Have you ever heard of the Trail of Tears?" Dodge asked as he kicked the stand and dismounted the bike. He reached out a hand to help me off.

I took off the helmet and shook my curls out. One advantage to my hair was I only had to run my hands through it a few times to get it to settle the way I liked it. With the braids Tambre put in, plus her magic conditioner, I was set. "I remember hearing about it in school. Something about Native Americans being forced to leave their lands and relocate. A lot of them died."

Dodge nodded. "Happened in a bunch of states. Alabama, Florida, Georgia, North Carolina. Tsali, his family, and a whole bunch of Cherokee hid in the mountains to keep from being moved. The army tried for years but never found them. There's a lot to the story, but it ends when Tsali and his sons give themselves up on the promise that the rest of the hiding Cherokee would go free to live their lives."

He nodded to some markings on one boulder. "I found it years ago when I needed a break to get away from my life. Between Mallory and my dad, sometimes I got pulled into their drama whether or not I liked it. Hell, I still get pulled in now. There's a peace in this place I needed and still need. I come out here and sit on the rocks where I imagined the artist sat. I listen to the sounds of the woods and think about my place in it."

The crude pictures were faded but still clear enough. Three very realistic stick figures that depicted an adult and two children with bows and arrows drawn. They chased a deer that looked to be running. A bird flew overhead, wings out straight and beak pointed to a round sun. I was in awe. "That's so cool. How old is it?"

Dodge shrugged as he pulled himself onto a flat area. I had the impression he'd done this many times. "No clue, sweetness. Could be from the time of Tsali.

Could be some Boy Scout earning a badge. All I know is this is a good place to hide from the world for a little while." He reached out a hand to pull me up next to him. "We can't run from ourselves or the problems we face, but it doesn't hurt to take a break when you need one. Just quiet down and listen."

The smooth surface of the rock was cool with a light covering of damp moss. I sat next to Dodge anyway and took his advice.

Getting out of my head was harder than I thought. The conversation with my mother still rang in my ears, and that hurt continued to radiate through my chest. I closed my eyes at the remembered pain and let it wash through me.

Gradually, I became aware of other senses. A bird chirped somewhere in the distance, and another one answered. Wind whispered through the trees, making them creak. I inhaled the clean scent of pine, the earthiness of decaying leaves, the sweetness of pure air, and did like Elsa advised.

I let it go.

"Look up, baby, but don't make any sudden moves or noise."

I opened my eyes, not sure what he referred to, and saw it. A deer, standing not ten feet away. It wasn't as big as I thought it would be, though the pointy rack of antlers on its head made up for any lack of size, and its coat had a reddish tan color. It snuffled at the ground, then paused and raised its regal head to stare at us.

I held my breath. The animal's velvety brown eyes looked into mine, and I had the distinct impression that I was in the presence of royalty. Then it licked its nose and sauntered off, white tail flicking as it moved.

Wow. Just wow. I blew out a slow breath and turned my head to see Dodge's reaction to the forest visitor.

What did he do?

He kissed me.

Slowly.

Thoroughly.

Worshipfully.

His lips were warm and soft as they pressed gently against mine. Whatever this man's status on paper, there was no doubt he was mine.

And I was his.

"Love is never a sin."

The words came back to me as I moved to straddle his lap. The hard evidence of his desire nestled between my legs, and I rubbed against it. His groan filled my mouth as he lifted his hips to press against me.

"Fauna," he breathed in reverence. "I filed for

divorce this morning before coming here. It's long overdue. I took the papers to the courthouse when it opened. I'm letting go of the past and looking forward to a new future. I want it to be with you." He gave a little sardonic laugh. "I had this whole speech prepared with a list of reasons why we should be together and how you needed to forgive me, but I forgot about it the moment I saw you crying."

"I don't care about your reasons. I need you to make love to me. Right here, right now."

His eyes darkened, and his body tensed beneath mine. "It's a little rough for our first time. You sure you want that here?"

A thrill ran through me that he wasn't pulling away from the idea. "I think it's perfect."

I hadn't dressed for seduction, but I did have on my favorite pair of panties, the ones with the cute bow. I lifted my shirt over my head, taking my sports bra with it. His hands trailed down my back as I arched into his touch. His lips found their way to my breast, and he suckled me, his tongue tracing over my nipple before drawing it into his mouth. His tugs and pulls burned through to my pussy, and I ground myself on him even harder.

Too many clothes. We had too many clothes on. It was warm. The sun was bright. Why weren't we naked already?

I pulled at his shirt, and he shed his cut first before I raised the hem halfway. I remembered that beautiful body of his from the hotel. Perfectly formed pecs under heavy shoulders. I ran my palms over those flat slabs of hard muscle before lowering my head to kiss him again. His movements got bolder as he sought my tongue with his. I slid off the rock and pulled my leggings off, dropping my underwear with them. My legs were shaved, but I'd not done any other grooming in a while.

"I let it grow back. Hope that's okay."

His answer was to switch places with me and lift me onto the sun-warmed rock. The flattened area was large enough for me to lean back as he spread my legs wide. I felt air hit my pussy for a brief moment before his mouth came down on me.

I let out a cry as he didn't waste any time playing around. He zeroed in on my clit, sucking, circling, teasing, setting off starter sparks in my belly and putting me on a slow braise. This was what he'd done for me so many months ago, and I reveled in the feel of it again. My fingers threaded through his thick hair as he fed from me. Sounds came from my throat as I drew nearer to climax.

"Dodge, I'm so close."

Then I was there. His tongue beat out a rapid tattoo, and I came with a long cry, my body spasming beneath his expert mouth. I remembered this from the hotel. He'd gone down on me twice, taking control and making me come so hard that my body had gone completely limp. I had a vague memory of passing out shortly after the second orgasm while I demanded a third. In this moment, I was only drunk on him and the fire he'd lit inside me. His mouth was magnificent, but this time, I wanted more.

I pushed him back and fumbled at his jeans button. His hands covered mine, and I noticed they were shaking.

"I don't have any condoms." His husky voice told me he was at his breaking point.

"I have an implant. We're good."

"I won't last long. It's been four or five years."

Whoa! Four or five years? That means he's been faithful to Mallory this whole time while she's been catting around. And he's going to break those vows for me?

"It's okay. I'm okay. I just really want to feel you inside me. Please don't stop this time."

I reached my prize. He was commando again, and I wondered if he even owned underwear. Long, thick, with a broad purple head, his cock pulsed in my grip. A bead of moisture collected at the top and ran down the front to drip over my fingers. I thought it was the most erotic thing I'd ever seen. To punctuate my point, I leaned forward and took him in my mouth, just the tip. His flavor, salty and sweet, dripped over my tongue. Dodge let out a harsh growl and went rigid. I slid him farther into my mouth.

"You keep that up, I won't make it much longer."

I lay back as he covered me, and my legs circled his hips. Sex outdoors on a big rock was awkward, and perhaps it *would* have been better to wait for a bed, but as that big cock slid inside of me, I decided our first time was perfect.

He filled me, his eyes on mine as he leaned over me, his teeth gritted as he fought to keep from coming too quickly. God, he felt so good, so right, so perfect. His hips nestled between my legs, and he let out a long, ragged breath when he was all the way inside. I shifted and squeezed my muscles around his thick girth, and he hissed.

"Fauna, I'm barely hanging on."

I smiled at him and did it again.

He came then. Not with a roar or a big show. He closed his eyes and let loose inside me with a lengthy sigh. His orgasm kept going as he waved and jetted once, twice, three times. His body trembled, and he laid his forehead to mine. "I'm sorry. I said I wouldn't last."

He was still hard even after coming.

"You've got nothing to be sorry for. This is what I

wanted, and you gave it to me. I'm counting on you giving it to me again and again."

His blue eyes opened, and I saw moisture in them. "I'll make it up to you."

Yes, he would. Neither of us was ready for the words yet, but I had no doubt they were coming. There were some challenges we had in legal form that he had to attend to before he fully committed to me in any real capacity. I supposed I should have had a problem with it, because technically he just broke his vows, but did it count when the other one did it first? Some people might take a dim view of us, but I wasn't so sure anymore.

Another challenge came with family. If my mother knew I was even thinking about dating a biker, she would hit the roof. She'd probably disown me. The narrow path she'd tried forcing me to walk all these years had no forks or variations, and the strained relationship we had would never improve unless I brought home a rich doctor, lawyer, or politician.

Then there was the race thing. He was all-American White, and I was not. Being mixed, I was still considered Black, but I'd been told I was too White to really be Black. It bothered me sometimes that I could be labeled and put in so many different boxes that had nothing to do with who I was. I'd spent a lot of my life dealing with prejudices I had no control over, but none of it seemed to matter to Dodge.

"Love is never a sin."

For the rest of my days on this earth, I would forever remember and be grateful for Tambre's words of wisdom.

The rock was getting uncomfortable under my bare ass. Dodge slid out of me and helped me up. I realized a problem I was going to have on the ride back—wetness from a combination of both of us ran down my inner thighs, and there was nothing I could do about it.

I wrinkled my nose as I slipped on my panties and leggings. Dodge came up to hug me from behind.

"I didn't plan this, but I'm happy it happened. Really fucking happy it did. Look, I can't tell what's coming around the bend for us, but I know there's shit I have to finish to make it right. That's what I wanted to talk to you about. I've made a decision, and it's time for me to take control of my life so I can have one with you. Can I ask you do to something for me? Can you be patient while I get it done?"

Like I have any other answer to give him. "Yes."

He smoothed a hand over my rumpled curls and kissed the top of my head. "I need to get back, and you do too. I'll come by after closing tonight?"

He voiced it as a question, but I recognized it as a statement. This man had become mine, and it felt right.

"Sounds good."

He kissed me again before handing me the gargantuan helmet.

I didn't need the words to recognize what this morning meant.

Dodge, a member of the Dragon Runners MC, had made me his old lady.

CHAPTER 27

Fall had peeked around the corner. Leaves were turning with red, yellow, and gold colors dotting the mountain landscape. I thought tourism would start waning, but if anything, it ramped higher. People flocked for those last few rafting trips and to see the changing season. The railroad was still going strong, and my restaurant was booming.

I found another assistant chef to add to my kitchen, which allowed me to expand my menu and take off one night a week. I also opened for a lunch buffet on weekends, and the response was phenomenal. The reviews poured in, earning me a 4.87-star rating. My restaurant appeared on the vacation travel sites as a place to visit.

One month. Four weeks of being Dodge's girlfriend. Old lady. Whatever. It was tough sometimes, as he worked mornings and afternoons, and I worked afternoons and evenings, but we made it happen. He came by the restaurant and sat at the bar with Macie. Dewey was there occasionally. I brought him lunch at the garage so often, Brick asked if I'd cook for him too.

Then there were the nights. Those wonderful nights I spent looking up into his brilliant blue eyes as he moved inside me. Sometimes he made love to me slow, building the tension until I was ready to combust. Other times he fucked me hard and fast, driving me insane. He loved to go down on me and did it often. Once, while we watched a Netflix series episode, he lay behind me on the sofa and played with my nipples the entire hour. Then he pulled off my leggings, spread me open, and made me come on his tongue while the closing credits rolled. The man had no modesty and paraded buck-ass naked around whoever's place we spent the night at. I didn't think that was bad, as his body was a magnificent specimen of maleness.

I stayed with him a few times a week up at the Lair. Now, I was no longer a guest; I was family. I met more of the club members and their wives. Betsey introduced me to her grandchildren and the children of the others. She was grandma to all of them, which I thought was the coolest. She reminded me of my own grandmother, the one who left me the box of costume jewelry. I talked with Katrina over her swelling stomach and found out she and Mute were having a boy. I spent time holding Cameron, Table and Lori's newborn son. She told me her story about how she wasn't sure she could get pregnant after the abuse she suffered and thought her beautiful step-daughter might be her only child. Eva and Stud had been a baby-making factory with their quintet of cute blonde girls.

No one said squat to me about Mallory and Dodge's marital status. Either they didn't know or didn't care. As far as the Dragon Runners MC was concerned, I was Dodge's woman, and he was my man.

I tried hard, but there wasn't any other time in my life that I could say I was this happy.

So of course, something had to come spoil it.

Dinner service concluded for the evening. It was a Thursday night, and the tables turned at least three times between the hours of four and eight thirty. Most people had cleared out by nine, and I was waiting at the bar for Dodge to come get me for a night at the Lair. My people were in charge of cleanup tonight so I could leave earlier than normal. Dewey came into town that day and was hanging at the bar as well.

"Your restaurant is really nice." He poked his glasses up on his nose. He wasn't particularly social and didn't stand out like Macie, who loved to wear full makeup when working. Plain clothes, plain hairstyle—Dewey was just plain. It was hard for me to see Macie with this man, but they were together, and it seemed to be working out so far. I hoped this was a good thing for my best friend.

"Thanks, D. I really appreciate you helping."

His cheeks flooded with color, and he dropped his eyes. I barely heard his murmured "You're welcome."

Two arms came around me, and I was pulled back into a hard body that smelled faintly of orange and car engine grease. "Hey, sweetness. I need a shower somethin' fierce. Mind if I go upstairs first?"

I grinned. "I'll come with you. Macie? Dewey? I'll leave you to it."

"Make sure and check behind his ears," Macie trilled. "Plus any other crevices or cracks."

Dodge coughed a laugh, and I rolled my eyes. "Say good night, Macie."

"Good night, Macie!"

Up in my apartment, Dodge stripped bare and stepped into the tiny stall. I wished I could have joined him, but there was no way I would fit too. He left the curtain open, so at least I got a show while he soaped up using one of the fragrant lavender bars I'd bought from Psalm's store. Suds covered his body, ran down his rounded pecs, over his washboard abs, and trickled down sturdy thighs. He worked up a serious lather on his head with a squirt of my shampoo, and I wished like hell my shower was bigger.

His dick hung between his legs. Earlier this week, I'd asked him to shave me again. He did and gave me a long orgasm afterward, his tongue teasing my bare pussy. Then he told me to do the same to him. I carefully worked the trimmer around his balls before taking him in my mouth and making him come. I had to use my hands as I couldn't take all of him at once. Remembering the sounds he made as he reached climax, I wanted to do it again.

I cleared my throat. "Do you even own underwear?"

He chuckled as he rinsed his head. "Yeah, but I've gotten used to not wearing it. There were times as I kid when I didn't have any clean ones or anything that fit, so I got into the habit of going commando. Now it feels weird to have anything on. I'll put on a pair of boxers if I'm gonna be in and out of coveralls in the paint booth, but most of the time, they stay in the drawer."

He maneuvered the spray to get the rest of the soap off his body. "Does it bother you?"

I caught sight of his sculpted ass. "Nope. Not in the least. Just curious."

"Curious enough to come over here?"

I laughed. "You'll get me all wet."

"Oh, sweetness, I hope so." I could hear the grin in his voice.

Turning to face me, he placed a hand on his dick now sitting at half-mast and began stroking himself. The sight was mesmerizing. I licked my lips, and his fist tightened.

That was all I needed. I tore off a button in my haste to get my chef's coat off, then dropped it to the floor. My shoes, socks, pants, shirt, bra, and panties followed in short order. If we got water all over the floor, we'd deal with it later. I dropped to my knees just outside the stall and took that giant head between my lips.

I could only get half of his length in my mouth, so I worked the base with my hand. He stood still, letting me control the movement and speed. I raised my eyes to see his staring down at me, taking him in, my mouth and cheeks stretched around him. His pupils dilated, and his breathing grew faster and harsher.

"Fuck, baby. Stand up and turn around."

I did, and he pulled me back to meet his slick body. One hand cupped my breast, and the other lifted my leg before his fingers slid through my wet pussy. "I want to try something. You game?"

Am I game? Absolutely.

"Bend over in front of me, hands on the floor. Got it? I'm gonna lift you now. Spread your legs and put them around my waist."

My arms were strong as I planted them. There was no hesitation when he placed his hands securely under my hips and pulled them up. My thighs wrapped around him, and his cock found me. In this position, I had very little control. He penetrated me, sinking deep into my body.

"I love watching you take me," he groaned as he drew back a bit before pushing in again.

Me? I had no words, only gasps as he filled me. Then filled more. The depth, speed, and strength of his thrusts varied, and he was the one to make it happen. I just hung here practically upside down as he did all the work. My focus was solely on what was happening between my legs. Fire. Ice. Burn. Freeze. It was there, but I had no say in how fast it came. Several shallow thrusts, then a long, full, hard one. He was teasing me with his dick.

The orgasm hit me as a surprise. I hadn't realized I was that close. My body spasmed, and I had to remember to keep myself steady so as to not fall to the floor. Another wave came, though maybe just a continuation of the first, but it rolled over me as Dodge yelled his own pleasure. He pushed in, pressing as far as he could go, filling me so completely that I couldn't tell us apart.

When I was back on my feet, Dodge lifted me again, my legs dangling as he kissed me. "Where did you learn how to do that?" I asked.

He smiled against my lips. "Imagination." He kissed me again. "And an internet search. It's called a wheelbarrow. I got a whole folder of positions—"

"Dearest darlings, I hate to interrupt your happy-slappy time, but there's a problem down here you need to take care of."

Macie's voice echoed up the staircase and had the effect of an ice-cold shower. Why was he still here when I was sure he'd said goodbye and left? I threw on my clothes and hurried down the stairs to the restaurant. I heard the raised voice before I got to the bottom, and my blood started simmering.

Chase had come for a visit. He stood in the doorway of my walk-in fridge and glared at me as he slammed the door shut. Then he stomped into my kitchen and started opening my cabinets. He had an older man with him who was on the tubby side with a ponytail of long hair on the back of his balding head. He was trying to reason with Chase but not getting anywhere.

"Dude, there are no violations here. It's clean as a whistle."

"Check the pantry," Chase ordered.

"I'm telling you there's nothing here."

Dewey stood just outside the doorway that led from the kitchen to the dining area. I called to him first. "Hey, D? Is anyone else still out there?"

He shook his head and acted as if he wanted to melt into the floor. "Only me and Macie. These two got here just as we were leaving and banged on the door until we let them in."

No customers left. Good deal. Now I could let loose. "Chase, what the fuck are you doing here?"

"Health inspection. You got permits for all this?"

What the fuck? "Of course I do, you idiot. They inspected me at the beginning of the month." I pointed to the A inspection grade sticker on the wall. "What's your point? Trying to shut me down?"

Of course he was. Of all the fucked-up shit he'd pulled on me, this was by far the worst. How had I ever dated him?

"A local woman posted that she saw mouse turds on the floor," he stated as he jerked a drawer open. Part of me felt violated as he poked around the utensils. Another part of me was mad as hell.

"Who?" Outrage filled me.

"I don't know. I found it on a review website."

"So you're trolling for shit about my restaurant now. Real mature, asshole." I turned to the other man. "And who are you?"

The tubby guy grunted and ran a hand over his bald spot. "I'm a health inspector for the state based out of Asheville. Cormer is the guy for this area, but he's on vacation. Chase here came to the office this week and kept pushing until my supervisor sent me out here for a surprise inspection." He shrugged and tapped the iPad in his hand. "I haven't found anything that's not up to code. It's all spit-shine clean. Everything is labeled and in order. No mold, no trash, no bugs, no mice." He grinned and gave me a weird thumbs-up. "You got it goin' on, dude."

"I found it," Macie announced, his fingers tapping across his phone. "The review. It's on sound-offaboutit.com. It's that whacked-out conspiracy site people use to bitch about anything and everything."

The inspector peered at the screen and knitted his brows together. "Yessiree, those are mouse turds, but that ain't at the Smoky Mountain Bistro. That's from the *Rocky* Mountain Bistro in Colorado. You got the wrong place, genius."

"No I didn't," Chase sneered. "Go check the store-room, Mike. I bet that's where they are."

"How 'bout you stay where you are." Dodge had

joined the party. He turned to Chase. "You need to get gone and stay gone."

A big belly whoosh hit me. Not fifteen minutes ago, this man made me come with vaginal penetration only, something that rarely happened in my world, yet I was turned on again big-time by this caveman-protect-my-woman behavior.

Chase saw it, too, and stepped back. I recalled the last time these two met, when Chase had ended up bent over with his arm twisted behind his back. "You're not in charge of me!"

An image rose in my mind of Chase in a diaper with a rattle in his hand. I bit my lip to keep from laughing. This situation wasn't particularly funny, but a grown man acting like a toddler was.

"Dude, I'm telling you, there's nothing here. We're talking A plus-plus-plus. I'm going home." Mike turned to me. "Sorry for all trouble."

Chase spluttered, "You can't leave now!"

Apparently even this laid-back man had a shenanigans limit. "Watch me, dude. You want a ride back to Asheville, you better come quick. I missed my favorite hot yoga class at the Yoga Spot tonight because of this shit."

"This isn't over," Chase huffed at me.

"Why?" This came from a sardonic Dodge. "Why isn't it over? You broke up. Fauna moved on. Whatever competition you think this is, it's done. Build a fucking bridge and get over it."

I let out a giggle when I heard one of my favorite sayings.

Macie's reaction beat mine. He burst into big hysterical laughs and made a huge show of it. "Ah! Build a fucking bridge! Oh my Lord! Ah! Dude! I can't breathe!"

"Go to hell, Macie," Chase snapped.

"Suck a dick, asshole." Macie wiped his eyes and kept laughing. "You're just jealous you got beat by a Black woman."

Oh yeah, he went there. I wasn't going to say that part out loud, but that idea had cropped up a time or two in the back of my head. I dated this man at one time and thought I loved him. Now, I believed he used me to get to his own goals.

"That's got nothing to do with it," Chase groused. His frantic drive when he first got here had disappeared. "No one will hire me anywhere in Asheville. My reputation is ruined thanks to her."

"Just go," I said. Fatigue hit me, and I wanted nothing more than to skip the Lair and go back upstairs to crash across my borrowed bed for the night.

A trickle of flow-back started between my legs from Dodge's attentions. *Bleh.* I hadn't done any cleanup before running down to answer Macie's summons. I loved having sex with Dodge, but the sticky part afterward was annoying. Dammit, I had on my favorite panties again! "You're welcome to find a job anywhere in the state of North Carolina. Hell, you're welcome to find a job anywhere in the whole damn country. Leave Bryson City to me."

"I'm gonna call the po-po," Macie declared and swiped at his phone.

"No need for police." Stud came in the kitchen, followed by Mute. A bright blond Viking god and a brooding dark Hades. Their presence brought a finality to this cute little drama my ex tried to throw. "There's a guy waiting for you outside. I think you're done here."

Chase opened and closed his mouth like a stranded guppy a few times, but he couldn't find anything to say. Finally, he stuck his nose in the air and looked down on me. "You'll fail. Maybe not tonight, but you'll fail."

I swear Mute growled, and Chase practically ran out the door.

"I just died and went to hot mountain man heaven," Macie breathed in reverence as he fanned himself. "Dewey and I need to get a motorcycle."

I laughed. "Where is Dewey?"

Macie waved his hand in the air. "Oh, he left a

little while ago. He can't take any kind of confrontation. He grew up in a lotta family drama and can't stand it."

"We need to go too. River's Edge is open, and I'm late for a set. Betsey's up at the Lair tonight with her grandkids. Kat isn't working there because of her pregnancy, which leaves Bruiser and Mute to run the bar," Stud explained. "If dumbass doesn't get a clue this time, let me know and I'll file a harassment claim and get a restraining order."

I was getting really uncomfortable and trying not to fidget as I thought about wet spots. "I'm sorry you had to come out."

Stud chuckled and gave me a half smile that rang church bells in my head. "No problem. Dodge could have handled it, but he texted for backup. Probably so he wouldn't beat the shit outta that guy."

Dodge came up behind me, one of his signature moves, and pulled me into his body. "Might as well get used to it, sweetness. You're in the Dragon Runners now."

CHAPTER 28

SOMETHING IN THE UNIVERSE WAS EITHER SKEWED OR God had a big sense of humor. Time seemed to move with a speed somewhere around frozen oil sludge. Dodge swore as another car limped into the parking area. Another flat tire emergency from a tourist. Brick lumbered out to meet the young couple and check out the problem. Dodge had already identified it—the front right tire was shredded, and the bent rim rested on the ground.

He glanced at the shop clock. The paint job he had in the booth was almost complete, but the normal workload was behind. Brick had asked him to fill in as able. A couple of oil changes, air filters, one head gasket, two battery and alternator combinations, and now a blown tire.

He wiped his hands on his coveralls and inhaled

a breath of gasoline-tainted air. "Almost six o'clock, boss man. This the last one?"

Brick nodded. "Yup. You planning on staying late to finish the Goat?"

"Nope. I have other plans."

The grunt Brick gave sounded rough. "I hope them plans include some papers and a visit to the courthouse."

Dodge smiled as he closed the hood of the car he'd just finished. "Filed them already. Just gotta wait for the hearing."

It had been absolute heaven since he and Fauna stopped fighting the attraction and got together. Last week's drama with Chase was put on the back shelf to be forgotten. He was at her restaurant almost every night, watching her run the kitchen with obsessive efficiency. She was demanding in her standards, and her staff followed her lead. Macie entertained from the bar and kept up the flow from the kitchen to the dining room.

Dodge was glad to see Katie Grace getting along so well after leaving Jimmy's. Rafter had been talking about the cute server at the bistro. Dodge both hoped and dreaded when the younger man finally found the guts to ask her out. He looked at Katie Grace as a sister and would personally bury anyone who messed with her.

After the workdays, he would take Fauna upstairs to her apartment, where he would make love to her with his mouth and body. True to his word, he did make it up to her and then some. He hid nothing from her and talked about his impending divorce openly.

"Mallory doesn't have to agree to it, but it's easier if she signs the papers. That is, when the sheriff finds her. If she wants to contest this, it'll make it longer and harder to get. I'm pretty sure if she does, I can make a good case for abandonment and infidelity. But I hope we don't have to go down that road."

He lay naked on his back after coming hard. Fauna curled into him and drew light patterns across his stomach and ribs. "Why did it take you so long to get this done?"

He blew out a breath. "After the first time she left me, I'd hoped we could work it out. After the second time, it was pretty clear she would never be the wife I needed, but I still felt responsible for her. She's been back and forth so many times, I lost track. Last few years, it's been mainly for insurance. I had her on my health plan and wanted to make sure she had coverage if she needed it. Didn't really have any other reason besides that, I suppose. I don't love her anymore, but taking care of her became a habit, I guess. I figured I'd get the legal done when the time was right."

His dick twitched to life as her hand moved lower. She

traced its burgeoning length, and he squirmed beneath her touch.

"Is it the right time now?" she asked in that husky tone of hers as she moved on top of him. He didn't think he would ever tire of hearing it. Her slick body welcomed him as she mounted open legged so he got a full view of his dick entering her.

"Absolutely, sweetness."

Dodge shook his head to clear it. Just the memory of that sight had him half hard.

He checked the sizes and pulled a tire from the stock in the back. The rim was a total loss, so he pulled one of those too. No need to put the car on a lift for a simple tire exchange. Brick had already put the portable jack under the vehicle when Stud came roaring up on his bike.

"We got a problem."

Brick was on alert instantly. "What happened? Betsey? The Lair?"

Stud shook his head. "The bistro. It happened in our town. Someone roofied Katie Grace."

What the fuck?

"Where's Mute?" Brick asked, his voice frigid.

"At the River's Edge. Betsey is on her way over right now. So is Blue."

Brick turned to the open garage bays and bellowed. "Forge, get over here and finish this tire.

Close it down after and get on over to the River's Edge. Stud, make sure Bruiser is on with Mute tonight. Tell Taz to lock down the Lair and get Molly and Tambre on standby up there. I want every Dragon Runner out at all the bars in town keepin' watch. Make assignments if you have to. We need a big show of force with our colors in full view. Whoever this asshole is, he picked the wrong place to fuck with. You spread the word—I want him before the law gets him. Dodge, come with me."

Fury rose in Dodge's gut. The bistro. Katie Grace. Fauna's business.

Fuck! Someone is going to die tonight.

"It gets worse," Stud stated.

Dodge spoke up, his voice almost as tight as Brick's. "Worse? How the fuck can it get worse?"

"They're saying that bartender friend of Fauna's is the one who did it."

BRICK AND DODGE HEADED OUT ON THEIR BIKES, motors running hot and high as they ignored the speed limit signs. An ambulance was pulled up at the front of the restaurant, and Dodge got a glimpse of a small body being loaded into the back. An oxygen mask covered her face, but Katie Grace's blonde hair was visible. Blue lights flashed everywhere, illuminating the faces of the onlookers, most of whom Dodge guessed came from the dining room.

"She was bringing us our plates when she just stumbled and fell."

"Hit her head too. Poor thing."

"I thought she was drunk."

"It was that gay feller. Only one behind the bar all night."

Dodge caught phrase after phrase as he dismounted and hurried to the door. An officer stopped him. It was all he could to do to keep from punching the man. "My girlfriend is in there."

"I get that, but so is all the evidence. Too many people in there right now is gonna stir shit up."

"Hang tight, brother," Brick gruffed. "I'm gonna go talk to Blue."

"You think Macie had something to do with this?"

Brick pursed his lips. "Hell no. By the looks of it, he's the one, but it don't make no sense. I've seen him and Katie Grace a time or two when I brought Betsey here for dinner. They were smilin' and cuttin' up like good friends. I cain't tell for sure, but I seem to recall him workin' on the night Zelda was killed. 'Sides, why would a gay man want to mess with a young girl? Especially one he's friends with and works with?" He tipped his head back and shook his head. "Like I said, it don't make no sense. Somethin' ain't right, but we ain't gonna figure it out in the next ten minutes. You go get to your girl. Imma head over to the station and see what's really going on."

Macie came out then, handcuffed and escorted by two grim-faced officers. He'd been crying with long streaked tears flowing down his cheeks. "I didn't put nothing in her water glass but a lime wedge. She likes lime over lemon. Crazy White girl!"

Dodge didn't believe for a nanosecond that Macie had anything to do with Katie Grace's condition. He ignored the orders from the deputy to stay away and walked over to the distraught man. "We know you didn't do anything, and we'll get you out as soon as we can."

"Dewey said he'd come bail me out in a little while. He came in to hang at the bar and wait for me to get off. We were going to go over to the casino after closing," the man wailed. "You just take care of Fauna and my little Gracie K. Oh God, I hope she's all right!"

Dodge finally got access to the restaurant. Fauna was in the back throwing out piles of food. After hearing about the possible drugging, no one wanted to eat anymore. Dish after dish was tossed violently into a big black trash can.

"They said it was okay to clean up. They already

took samples," Fauna groused as she dumped another plate and slapped it against the side of the can. "I don't know why. Katie Grace and the other servers didn't eat from customer plates. Macie has water glasses for them behind the bar. He's always done that for all the staff who work with him. The police took them as evidence."

A pile of sliced tomatoes landed with a splat, and the stainless steel pan they were in clattered as she lobbed it into the wash sink. "Katie Grace. Only Katie Grace got sick. Someone had to target her. I hope they find him soon. I hope… I hope…." Her frantic movements slowed down and her voice broke. "Fuck me, I hope she's gonna be okay."

Dodge's anger simmered below the surface, but he kept it in check. At least for now. "Brick is on it."

"I can't believe this is happening."

He moved and wrapped her in his arms. Tears flowed from her eyes, and she clung to him. "We're gonna get to the bottom of it, sweetness. Whoever this guy is, he better pray the police get him first. Even then, he might not be breathing by tomorrow morning. Katie Grace is well loved in this community, and Blue might wear a badge, but he's still a Dragon Runner."

"I love you."

His heart jumped at the impromptu confession.

He didn't expect it, but he'd take it. "I love you, too, sweetness."

She pulled back, and he regarded her splotchy face. "Do you love me enough to help me get the dishes done and close the place down? I want to get to the hospital, then go see Macie. I can't leave him in jail tonight."

"He said Dewey would come get him later." Dodge picked up a set of plates and scraped them into the bin.

"That's right. Dewey was here tonight. He said he liked my coq au vin. You should have heard the way he said it. I think he was trying to make a joke. I don't know where he is now, though."

"Plan B. We clean up and close up, then go to the hospital. Betsey is probably already there with Katie Grace's parents. After, we'll call the jail and see if Macie has been sprung. If not, we'll go get him. If there's a bond, I'm sure the Runners will cover it."

"You're gonna need to modify that plan." Weatherman appeared in the doorway. He'd been spending most of his days lately taking care of his mother as she dealt with chemo treatments. Dodge hadn't hung with him much at all, but when the call went out, everyone responded.

"What do you mean?"

"Mom is at the hospital right now getting an IV

drip for dehydration. I saw Katie Grace was admitted. Someone else got admitted recently too. Mallory is there in ICU as a Jane Doe."

The world tilted on its axis, and Dodge almost fell over. Mallie? ICU?

Before he processed that piece of news, another highly irate voice pierced the air.

"Fauna Somers, what have you done now?"

A speechless Dodge looked up to see a conservatively dressed Black woman with a severely tight bun on her head and snapping dark eyes.

Why does the world have to have such shit timing tonight?

Fauna's mother had come for a visit.

CHAPTER 29

OF ALL THE FUCKED-UP THINGS I HAD TO HANDLE today, my mother hadn't been on that list. Yet here she was in all her glory. Harriet Somers, in the flesh. My father wasn't with her, which was a small comfort, but dealing with my mom was bad enough.

I was by myself with my mother strolling casually around my place. Dodge stood by me when she made her appearance, and she dismissed his presence almost immediately. He just had a major dumpage laid on him after a messy night, yet he still stayed with me until I shooed him out the door.

"You need to go take care of business at the hospital."

He pressed his lips together and inhaled sharply through his nose. I recognized the signal that he was worried. "I don't want to leave you alone right now."

Warm fuzzies bloomed in my belly at the thought that

he would rather stay with me and have my back than go deal with the recent shitstorm. But he was needed elsewhere. Trust started at the beginning, and if we were to make a go of it, I had to believe he'd come back to me. "I'm good. I got this. Go where you're needed most and keep me informed. I'll see you later?"

"I'll come home as soon as I can."

Home. That sounded so damn good, even if it was more of a squatter's crash pad upstairs than a real place.

"Who was that man? The one with the vest?" my mom asked.

"It's called a cut, and it shows he's a member of the Dragon Runners MC. His name is Dodge."

"What's an MC?"

"Motorcycle club."

Her nose wrinkled as she turned to face me. "He's a biker? Really, Fauna, I thought you had better taste than that."

"He's a good man. He spent a lot of hours helping me revamp this place." That was an understatement for all the work he and I poured into the renovations.

My mother gave a dismissive "Hmph" as she turned back to my dining room. I saw the clean booths, refinished floors, my snazzy custom-built bar, cute tables and chairs, fine artwork on the brick walls, and hanging Tiffany-style lamp shades adding their colors.

Apparently, my mother saw shit. "Rather generic."

I steeled my spine. Our last conversation didn't end well, and I expected this one wouldn't either. "I got most of the stuff used from a chain place."

"Secondhand?" I didn't have to see the eye roll to know she'd done it. "Surely you could have done better than that."

I ground my molars together in an effort to keep my mouth closed. "It fits the area, and I'm on a strict budget." *Need I remind you about your statement of not helping me get a business loan from dear old dad's bank?*

"Your menu looks nice, at least."

I wanted to scream. Katie Grace was at the hospital, the police were sorting through food samples and other stuff they collected earlier, Macie was at the station, and Mallory was in ICU. But I guess my menu was nice, and that made it all better. "Thanks. Mom, I have a lot going on right now. Why are you here?"

She turned to face me. "A few of the ladies at the club asked me about your place. I couldn't tell them much and didn't want to lie in case they ever came here."

What? "Your timing sucks."

She raised a perfectly formed eyebrow. "I gathered. What was it? Food poisoning?"

Rage flamed through me at her words, but somehow I managed not to lose it. I wanted to, but I held on to my control with my fingernails. "Not exactly. Local news is there's a serial rapist who's been drugging and assaulting women in bars. They've been trying to catch him for a while. So far, he'd stayed away from Bryson City, but apparently that's over. One of my servers was roofied this evening—or allegedly roofied. She's at the hospital. The police were here investigating." A now-familiar burn started in my sinuses.

Another "Hmph" was her only comment. It pissed me off.

"My kitchen sanitation is excellent. Always has been. Food poisoning will never be a possibility in my restaurant." My words came out like bullets, fast and spitting shells. I should have expected her to go there before all other possibilities. Everything in life was my fault, right?

She paused in front of a local artist's painting. The scene was from a popular overhang somewhere in the Smokies. A sea of black-and-gray mountains rose like cold sentinels as they guarded a rising sun. A thin line of bursting colors shone through a foggy covering, revealing the faint greens of pine trees. One of my favorites. I hadn't seen that particular place, but I hoped Dodge knew where it was and would take me sometime. My furnishings might be generic, but my artwork was kickass.

My mother regarded the painting before moving on to a display of local pottery. Some hermit guy who seldom if ever came down from his hideaway. I was getting more and more irritated. "Again, Mom, why are you here? Inspection? Been there, done that. Making sure I don't embarrass you further?"

"Oh for heaven's sake, Fauna. Can you please cut the drama?"

Fuck me, how many times had I heard that exact phrase? *"Cut the drama. Stop acting out. Why can't you be like your brother?"*

I wasn't proud to say it, but I lost my shit.

"Cut the drama? How can I do that, Mom? My whole fucking life has been drama. My grades were never quite good enough for you. You made a big deal of my friends back then because they weren't rich white-collar people. I never got to wear braids. You've hated my profession, something I'm passionate about. Any mistake or slipup you consider criminal. And now you come here, to my restaurant, *my* restaurant, on a night when I have a shit ton of stuff to handle to tell me it's generic and that I've poisoned someone. How the fuck am I supposed to react to that? As far as I can tell, I'll never be good enough for you or your fucking space shuttle high standards."

"How dare you speak to me that way? I'm your mother!"

"Biologically. I'm not really sure why you even had me."

"Because of your father!"

That shut me up. I'd never seen or heard my mother scream in that banshee voice before. Her main goal was keeping herself under strict control, tight and unrelenting. She could filet someone to the bone with precise, razor-sharp words. Not in ear-shattering shrieks. This woman in front of me had no resemblance to the one I grew up with.

My father? He and I had never had a close relationship and probably never would. He doted on his proud surgeon son but pretty much ignored his daughter. Resented me even, although as I kid, I never understood why. Did my mom push me so hard to get him to love me?

I might have had some sympathy for her, but she kept talking, and as she did, my heart grew cold.

"I met your father in college when he was in his rebellious stage. I had to go to Durham Tech because my parents were blue-collar workers and couldn't afford anything else. I waited tables at a wings and bar joint just to afford books. I wanted to go to Duke. That was *my* dream." She thumped her chest. "Finding a rich man to take care of me so I wouldn't have to wipe up crumbs, congealed hot sauce, and beer spills ever again. I met him when his fraternity brothers came to the wings place. He liked me well enough, but the big attraction was the thrill he got showing me off to his family. They hated the thought of him being with a Black woman as much as my family hated me being with a White man. The more they did to keep us apart, the more he was determined to parade me in front of them like a trophy. They tolerated me for the most part, saying it was just a phase, but then I got pregnant with your brother."

Her smile turned nasty. "He wanted me to abort, but I refused. An illegitimate child is worse than a mixed child in the eyes of the Somers family. He went through with the marriage, even though he was already catting around. When your brother was born, it was a relief to see him look more like his father than me."

This was true. My brother had more of Dad's DNA than I did.

I had no clue my mother went through all of this. Then again, I'd never witnessed any true affection between my parents. Family meals, when we had them, were stilted and cold.

"I did everything I could to fit in the Somers mold. The right hair and clothes, the right speech, the right social groups. No room for errors or mistakes or emotions. Your brother was perfect in school. Top grades, top honors, top awards. In the end it wasn't enough. Your father had his mistresses, and I found out he was planning on leaving me to be with one. That's when I got pregnant with you. In that circle, he could leave a wife and one child, and no one would blink an eye. Two would have made it harder. Three would have been impossible. I was planning on having a third child, but when you came out the way you did, that was it. He wouldn't touch me."

My heart bled. "So I was an insurance policy."

She ignored my statement. "He was heading to the CEO desk and didn't need any scandals or bad press. The banking industry is as cutthroat as any other business, and your father had to be aboveboard in all things. Including his marriage to me." She laughed. "Some people regarded us as the perfect modern couple, and being with me might have helped cata-pult your father into that presidential chair."

Very few times in my life, I had no words. No snappy rebound to say or flippant response. Betrayal sat heavy in my heart. I wasn't a wanted child. Just a tool for my mom to keep her spot among the rich folk. Part of me understood the struggle, as I'd dealt with the same ones myself, but the overwhelming sense of wrongness was more than I could take.

I waited for the pain to come, but it didn't. Instead, I had an almost euphoric sense of relief. I should have been reeling or collapsing on the floor in heartfelt agony, but for the first time ever, I felt…

Free.

"You came to check on me, and you did. You can leave now."

Her face fell as if she'd figured out what she said to me not thirty seconds ago and was regretting it. "Fauna—"

"You really should leave."

"I didn't mean—"

"I don't give a shit."

"Don't—"

"Stop." I barked the command louder than I'd ever spoken to her before. "I'm done. So fucking done. Despite what happened tonight, I have a thriving, growing business that *I* started. *Me.* No help from my family. Not one word of encouragement or support. I'm in a community that doesn't use me or judge me."

She scoffed as I knew she would. "Who? The

biker gang that man belongs to?"

I shook my head. "Not a gang. A club. No, that's not right either. The Dragon Runners are a family. *My* family now." Tears filled my eyes, but I refused to let them fall in front of this woman. This stranger. "They've had my back from the moment I set foot in this town. Betsey, Tambre, all of them. Dodge is a lot more than 'that man.' He's *my* man. My old man. I'm gonna put a ring on that big finger of his, and when we have kids, Betsey will be their grandma."

"Fauna, you will not marry that man."

Fuck me, Harriet was either deaf or insanely obtuse. I couldn't think of her as Mom or Mother anymore.

"You don't get a vote. As I already said, you can leave now. I have someplace to be, and you're not invited."

"You'll regret this. Your trust fund—"

"Fuck the trust fund. Keep it. Spend it. Burn it. I'll make my own way as I always have."

"Fauna, I'm warning—"

"I've been polite and asked nicely twice. Now I'm just gonna say it. Get the fuck outta my restaurant, and do not come back!"

She opened her mouth again, but whatever she wanted to say, I didn't hear it. I turned and walked away, heading back to my kitchen where I was the most comfortable. The pots and pans were hanging up ready for the next service. The grill was spotless, the prep area clean and everything in its proper place.

Including me. This was where I belonged. I really had no regrets about the breakup of me and Harriet. I assumed that meant my brother and father would also cease the little contact they had with me. I wasn't torn up about it.

"You feed people."

"There's something special about feeding hungry people."

Tambre's words echoed in my head and heart. Yes, I did. I fed hungry people, and I did it damn well.

"Everyone has challenges, some more than others, but I think it's how we face them and who we face them with that counts."

"Don't let small-minded people keep you from having all the happiness this life has to offer. That includes family."

A past conversation with Betsey followed close behind. She'd barreled into my life with a determination to be my friend, even when I didn't want one.

"I look at that as my obligation to pass on my blessings to people who need them the most."

"It's a big deal for a real biker to allow someone to ride with him. Means he's got respect and care."

My favorite bit of Runner Lady wisdom came to me as I thought about Dodge.

"Love is never a sin."

I decided my first tattoo would be that phrase on my forearm. I'd met Table, the club tattoo guy, and his wife at one of the Lair gatherings. Big, bald, and hot as all get-out, he only had eyes for the woman at his side. I was so going to do it as soon as I could.

A text buzzed my phone.

> Dodge: Katie Grace will be fine. She's got a big goose egg where she hit the floor but no concussion. They're letting her sleep now, but if you want to come see her anyway, I'll come get you. You okay?

I smiled and texted back.

> Me: I'm good. Real good. Talk about it later. Harriet is gone in more ways than one. I'll go see KG tomorrow.

> Dodge: Stud is our lawyer and is working on getting Macie out. He's not been charged yet and might be let go. Blue is with him now. Dewey said he can't swing it for a few days. He came to the jailhouse but didn't stay long.

I noticed he hadn't mentioned Mallory, and I decided not to bring it up.

Me: I guess there's nothing for me to do after all. Are you coming home soon?

Dodge: On my way. Love you, sweetness.

CHAPTER 30

Blue sat across from Macie in the interrogation room. The protocol was to keep prisoners in handcuffs, but he ignored that rule and took them off. The room itself was intimidating enough. Blank gray walls, heavy table bolted to the floor, and the most uncomfortable chairs known to man. A deputy stood near the locked door.

Macie slumped over, leaning on his elbows and sniffling. His eyes were swollen with big raccoon stains underneath where his mascara had smeared. Blue's thoughts had followed the same path as his father's. Macie as a serial rapist made no sense. None. Still, he had to go through procedure.

Stud sat next to Macie as his lawyer. To say this was awkward was an understatement, but they'd been here before. Blue had to keep everything as close to the book as possible because of all the cross connections to the club. Family was family, but business was business, and the two concepts needed to be separated.

"Tell me what happened as best as you can remember about tonight's work. Start from when Katie Grace got there for her shift."

Macie sniffed and blew out a haggard breath. "I'm always there early for prep. Gracie K showed up around three like she always does."

"Gracie K?"

Macie gave a short laugh. "I messed her name up the first time I met her. Katie Grace. Gracie K. She thought it was cute, so I kept doin' it. We call ourselves Macie-Gracie 'cause of how well we work together. Best server ever." He looked up from the table. "How is she? Anyone check on her?"

Stud answered. "Hospital said she's gonna be fine."

Fresh tears appeared in Macie's eyes. "Oh, thank the Lord for that. I can't handle anything bad happenin' to my little Gracie K."

Blue and Stud shared a glance. Nope, this was not the man they wanted.

"You got through prep. Any arguments or disagreements? Anything you two got mad at each other about?"

"No. Nothing. I stock the bar while she gets the dining room ready for people. Silverware, napkins, makes sure the table condiments are full. She does the assignment areas for other servers and brings them to me to check over. During service, she does a lot of the hostess work, like seating people and taking money. We joke around a lot. Have to, especially when it gets going." Macie laughed out loud. "Wanna hear what that little girl did? Burna Jones came in last week, all full of piss and fire 'bout somethin'. Didn't like the plates, didn't like the napkins, didn't like salmon but ordered it anyway. Didn't like the sauces. Lord, she had Gracie running all over the place. When Burna finally went up to pay, she started in again, saying how she saw Gracie lick her fingers before picking up a cookie to put on top of an ice cream dessert. Gracie didn't miss a beat. She smiled at that ol' battleax and said just as sweet as sugar, 'No ma'am, I wasn't licking my fingers. I was picking my nose.'"

Stud burst into laughter along with Macie, and Blue had a hard time keeping a straight face. They well knew Burna in the community for her sour disposition to everything and everyone.

"Anything like that happen tonight?" Blue asked.

Macie sobered up. "No. No glitches other than a heavy service. The tables turned three to four times.

Just as soon as one party left, another one got seated. We're still shorthanded, and it's all hands on deck to make things run smooth. There was a table of women who ordered a shit ton of mojitos. I made drinks like a madman, and Gracie K ran them as fast as she could, then boom, she went down like a sack of potatoes."

"The doctors said she ingested the drug. You have water at the bar for the waitresses. Tell me about that."

Macie wiped his eyes again, and Stud handed him a tissue. "We call them servers. It's a lot of work serving people, and I need to keep my staff hydrated. I keep glasses for them behind the bar along with a pitcher of ice water. That way they can get it themselves if I'm covered up. I make sure the pitcher is always full."

He shook his head. "It's just water, I swear. I poured my girl a big ol' glass and added a slice of lime to it. Other servers drank water I poured from the same pitcher. No one else got sick."

"Did anyone else get a lime?"

Macie shook his head. "A couple of them like lemon wedges, but Gracie K prefers lime. You think that was it?"

Stud frowned. "Hold up. Did the mojitos have lime in them?"

"Of course they did. Three sprigs of fresh mint crushed on the inside of a tall glass, two teaspoons sugar, three tablespoons lime juice, one and a half ounces club soda, chill with ice, garnish with lime slice and mint leaves. I increased everything by the pitcher."

Blue swiveled to the deputy. "Find out if anyone else came to the hospital tonight with signs of being disoriented or dizzy. If they didn't, they might just think they got drunk instead of drugged. Get samples of the limes over to the lab ASAP. I don't know if they can find anything or not, but it's a lead."

Macie raised a hand to his mouth. "Oh my God, you think there are more besides Gracie K?"

"I don't know. What can you tell me about the women who ordered the mojitos?"

Macie blew his nose. "One of them mentioned some sort of retreat group for single mamas. They're going rafting tomorrow. I don't know what company."

Blue's voice was grim as he gave more orders to the deputy. "Call Dennis and have him check his reservations. His is the closest raft tour place. Find those women ASAP." He turned back to fully face Macie and Stud. "Where does Fauna get her produce?"

"She buys local when she can, but some stuff she gets from a wholesaler in Asheville."

"Who has access to the food from when it arrives to when it's served?"

Macie let out an exasperated breath as his tears were replaced with frustration. "Just about everyone who works there. The kitchen staff, preppers, servers, me, and Fauna."

"Who cut the limes for the bar last night?"

"Gracie K. I ran out while I was fixin' all those mojitos, and she went back in the kitchen and cut them up for me."

Stud chuffed. "Well, she didn't roofie herself. Someone else had to have touched the produce first. Anyone in the kitchen staff you think might be a culprit?"

Macie snapped his fingers. "Chase was here a few nights ago. You remember him? Fauna's ex?" He faced Blue. "He blames her for getting him fired from the Omni and tried to do this bogus health inspection to get her shut down." He leaned back and crossed his arms. "He'd do anything he can to fuck with her."

Stud pursed his lips. "That's true. I met him when we picked up the restaurant furniture some months ago and again last week. What do you think, Blue?"

Blue sighed and tapped the legal pad with all of his notes. "There's motive, but it would be pretty damn hard for him to sneak into a walk-in fridge with a bunch of people working. There's also nothing to connect him with any of the other cases, but that's not my job right now. All I need to do is catch whoever hurt Gracie K." He shook his head to clear it. "Katie Grace. We'll start there and see where it leads."

CHAPTER 31

I was sure that people would stay away from a restaurant where a woman got drugged.

Totally. Fucking. Wrong.

The very next night I was flooded. Three nights later, people were still lined up before the doors opened for dinner service and didn't stop. The wait time increased to an hour or more. Instead of going to another restaurant, some parties put in their names and left to go explore the bookstore down the street, then came back before their names were called. Others ordered drinks at the bar and stood around, basically getting in the way. It was a skeleton crew, as I was down my best server and the bartender. Both Macie and I decided that even though he was free to go, there might be some backlash from the community and he should take some time off. Dewey had dumped him via text, which added another layer of shit on my best friend's back. Gay or straight, men could be real assholes. Macie had gone back to hang in Asheville with some friends for a while and lick his wounds, so to speak.

Who stepped in to help me? Betsey of all people. She didn't put on a show like Macie did by flipping caps and tossing bottles in the air, but simply her presence drew people in. She mixed drinks, dispensed conversation, and dropped some wisdom. All in her red hair and high heel boots glory.

I wanted to be her when I grew up.

The kitchen was subdued chaos for the first time, but we kept up. Dodge was over at the hospital. Katie Grace was home, but Mallory was still there, unconscious in the ICU. The assumption had been that she was another victim, but Blue did some investigating and learned some bad shit.

They had discovered Mallory outside a way off-track bar near Maggie Valley. Not a place for tourists, and from what Dodge described not really a bar. It was an old doublewide where drinks were served, but it was better known for shady deals, mostly in illegal moonshine so potent it would serve better for rocket fuel than consumption. According to the medical report, Mallory had a blood alcohol level of 0.13. Since

0.08 is considered being legally drunk, she was past that and probably headed to alcohol poisoning. The doctors said they couldn't tell if she'd been roofied in addition to the booze, but she had sex with someone before she stopped breathing. Several someones. There weren't signs of force, but whether the sex was consensual was up in the air. Of course, no one saw anything.

It was a sad situation, made worse by all the unknowns.

Guilt ate at Dodge, and there wasn't much I could do about it. He had no reason to feel that, but he'd been taking care of Mallory from childhood up 'til now in some form, and it got to him that she'd ended up this way. He was done with her and her shit, but he still visited the hospital since she had no one else to check on her. The other motivation was to inform her when she was on the mend and coherent enough to hear it that the divorce was real and it was time to move on.

"Lord have mercy, this is like them rubberneckers at a car accident on the highway. Everybody has to stop and look," Betsey announced as she clacked her way into the kitchen. Three empty pitchers were in her hands. The drinks? Mojitos.

Fuck me sideways.

It was the end of service, and most people had

gone home. I was glad, too, as I was exhausted. My kitchen crew were cleaning, and the servers were finishing up the dining room. I wiped down my station and stretched hard, several popping sounds coming from my back. "I can't tell you how much your help means to me. No way could I have handled these last few nights."

She dumped the pitchers in the soap sink where Felix was finishing up and flicked her nails—bright orange this time—at me. Her standard "Pssssht" response followed. "Runner women stick together. I might need some help myself someday, and I expect you to step up if it happens. You wanna make it up to me? Get Brick to eat more greens."

I laughed. It felt good to hear some humor. Dodge had joked about the kale battle between the patriarch and matriarch of the club. My mother—or rather, Harriet—hadn't contacted me, and I expected she never would. I tried texting my brother to see how the wind blew there, but I got a blocked message. So much for blood family.

"The trick for getting people to eat stuff they don't wanna eat is to cut it up in small pieces and mix it with other foods. Dodge said he didn't like mushrooms, but he ate them in the duxelles I made for the little stuffed appetizers. He loves them. I can make something similar like spanakopita. That's spinach-and-feta-stuffed phyllo triangles."

"Sounds good to me. Bring 'em to the Halloween barbecue at the end of the month."

Betsey picked up a couple of empty prep pans and took them to the dishwashing area. "I've handled big crowds at the River's Edge before, but this place? Lord have mercy. Anyway, I gotta get up to the Lair. Mute's over at the bar with Bruiser. Kat's not feeling real well, and I'm guessing we're gonna have us a new baby real soon. I'm gonna put my happy ass in a bed while I can."

She whirled a thick cape around her shoulders. She had on her Dragon Runners property cut and preferred the cape to a coat for the colder nighttime temperatures. My other kitchen help finished up the last of the dishes and got ready to leave himself.

I took a freshly washed glass and filled it with ice cubes. "Thanks, Felix. You can clock out if you're done."

The man nodded and left in short order.

I poured cold water from a filtered pitcher I kept in the kitchen and took a big gulp. The icy mix burned on the way down. Two of the servers came in back to log out of the timekeeper and wave goodbye. I followed them to the dining room and let them out the front door, locking up behind them.

It was down to me.

A ding on my phone indicated a text, and I swiped it open.

> Dodge: They're making me leave the hospital. I'd really like to be around people tonight. Mind meeting me at the Lair?

Did I mind? Absolutely not. Part of being in a relationship was taking care of each other. I'd never had that in its true sense until Dodge came in my life. He never had that with Mallory either, but I would do that for him now. He needed to be around family, and we'd go be around family.

> Me: No, baby, I don't mind at all. I'm almost done with closing. I'll come as soon as I can. You want me to come get you?

> Dodge: I've got my bike. Cold ride, but I could use a windy pick-me-up. See you there. Love you, sweetness.

> Me: Love you too.

I slipped the phone in my back pocket and turned off the lights. My lights. I grinned a little.

Back in the kitchen, I grabbed my water glass and downed the rest in one long cold gulp. There were a few dishes left in the drying rack, and I took a few minutes to put them away. I hung up my pots and pans, put away the rest of the utensils, and wiped up the sink. Felix had already mopped, and the floor showed a few damp spots left. I carefully stepped around them, then promptly grabbed at the counter as my feet went out from under me.

"Djammit," I muttered. My tongue felt thick and unwieldy in my mouth. My head spun as the world shifted and flipped over.

What the fuck?

I found myself on the floor. The white fluorescent tubes above me split and came back together just to split again. I closed my eyes at the scene and had the urge to vomit. My head lolled to the side, and I got a bird's-eye view of the underside of my prep counter. A lone papery onion skin sat a few inches from my face, and I had the absurd desire to blow it to see if it would fly.

Somewhere in the back of my mind, I recognized that someone had drugged me. I'd felt like this before. On a night months and months ago when I'd quit my job and woke up to find myself in bed with a man I didn't know.

A pair of flat, plain loafers appeared in my vision, blocking the sight of the onion skin. My numb lips formed a name, but before I said it, I was out.

CHAPTER 32

Dodge rolled into the Lair compound and parked his bike in the covered garage. Rain was in the forecast, and all the motorcycles were under cover for the night. Fauna would have to leave her car outside when she got here.

Fauna. His woman. His old lady. For the longest time, he'd thought he was destined to be single for the rest of his life, but then one night in Asheville changed all that. It was a fucked-up night, but the best one ever as long as it led to Fauna in his life. Forever.

The Lair was buzzing as usual. Drinking, music, and games punctuated by smiles, laughter, and comradery. Dodge spotted Weatherman arguing with a pretty blonde woman he'd never seen before.

Betsey had arrived moments before and was behind the bar. He had to remember to thank her for stepping in to help Fauna. Brick waved from his spot at the pool table. It was all good. It would be better when Fauna arrived.

Betsey opened a beer for him as he approached. "Thanks for everything. I'm sure Fauna has already talked to you."

She smiled as she popped the top. She inhaled as if preparing to say something, then let out a squeal. "Lord in heaven, Katie Grace! What are you doing here, child?"

Dodge turned with a big lump in his gut to see the cute girl hand in hand with a grinning Rafter. Soon, he would need to have a talk with the prospect.

"Is it okay that I'm here?"

Betsey pursed her lips. "I ain't servin' you if that's what you mean. You had a nasty experience just a few days ago, an' at twenty, you're still a minor for a few more months. Otherwise, come on in. How you feelin'?"

She perched on a stool at the bar, and Rafter stayed close by, hovering protectively. "I'm good. No aftereffects 'cept a bruise where I fell. I hope Fauna will let me come back to work soon. I heard the restaurant has been packed."

"Lord, yes. I've handled big crowds at the River's Edge, but I've always had Bruiser and other helpers. Macie must be a real artist to keep up with everything by himself."

Katie Grace giggled. "It does get bad sometimes. I thought Macie was gonna have a heart attack that night. I'm not allowed to mix drinks, but I can serve and help him with some prep." Her face dropped at the recent memory. "He freaked out when he couldn't find the slicer he likes to use for the drink garnishes. He had the wedger but not the slicer. Dewey had to help me look for it."

A tickle buzzed in the back of Dodge's head. "Dewey was in the kitchen that night?"

The young girl nodded. "I did a bunch of limes first, and he carried them out to Macie while I did some lemons." Her eyes widened as she took in Dodge's face. "Did I do something wrong?"

Dodge ignored the question and whipped out his phone. "Betsey, can you call Blue? I'm gonna check on Fauna. She should be here by now."

Betsey said nothing but motioned for Brick as she dialed. Dodge didn't bother with a text but called Fauna directly. Their last communication was about twenty minutes ago. The tickle morphed into dread. Something wasn't right.

"I'm heading over to the bistro. Tell Blue to meet me there, yeah?"

"What's going on?" Brick asked as he joined the group.

"I got a real bad feeling, boss man."

CHAPTER 33

I woke up. Sort of. My head was still floaty, and my surroundings were surreal as if I were in a bubble. Was I standing or lying down? I couldn't tell. A pretty Tiffany lampshade hung over my head. My apartment? Maybe. Looked a little like the extra one from the restaurant I'd installed.

Random thoughts came to my mind. *Smoky Mountain fog. I should get a fog machine. Match the painting downstairs.*

God, I wanted to puke. That sounded like a good idea. I turned my head and started heaving.

My head snapped to the other side with a stinging slap. *Ouch! That fucking hurt.*

A face floated over mine. "Stoo-pid cunnnt."

Who is that? Sounded kinda familiar but like it

was from the bottom of an echoing well. *What the fuck is going on?*

The fog in my brain cleared a little. I was naked on my back with a man hovering over me. Dodge? Dodge wouldn't hit me. Plus, this was a little guy. A naked little guy. A naked little guy pumping his naked little dick, trying to make it hard. The blurry figure whimpered as he worked himself, but nothing was happening.

Fuck me sideways, is this fucker trying to fuck me?

Repetitious much? I laughed, but it came out more like a gurgle.

"Don't laugh at me!" the man spat and hit me again.

The pain helped me sober up more. The man's face came into focus briefly, and more adrenaline poured into my system as I stared at him in shock.

"D?"

He stopped frantically pulling at his limp dick and stared back. "I wish you hadn't woken up yet, Fauna."

This was not a comedy. I was on my back while a man I barely knew tried to rape me. *Fuck no.* "Ged the fuck off me, ash-ol." My words came out slurred as hell, but I was getting some control back. I pushed at him and batted my hands at his head.

"Slut. All you women. Think you can be a man. I'll show you who's a real man."

He tried to part my legs, but I instinctually clamped them together and drew my knees up hard. This was fortunate, as I nailed him right in the groin. A high-pitched scream came from his mouth, and he rolled off me to the floor, clutching his teeny-weeny injured peeny.

A rhyme? Fuck, I need to burn this drug out of my system.

I rolled over and fell off the bed on the opposite side. More pain woke me up further, and I tried to stand. The world tilted, and I splatted on the ground. I tried again, this time making it to my hands and knees. Dewey kept crying behind me as I crawled to the door. There were steps I had to deal with. I'd figure that out when I got there. Ride down, slide down, or glide down. *Dammit!*

The crying dissolved into whines and sniffles. I didn't dare take a peek back. All my focus and effort were on the door and reaching it.

A foot planted on my butt and pushed me flat.

"You made me do this."

Something wrapped around my neck. One of the extensions I used for my bedside table lamp? It really didn't matter as it pulled and jerked my neck back. I couldn't breathe. I gagged and coughed. My hands scrabbled at the cord, cutting into my skin, my fingernails scratching my flesh bloody as I tried to loosen the noose.

Fuck me, I'm going to die.

Dodge would find my naked body and would be devastated. Macie would have a hard time too. My restaurant would fall into disrepair and go back to the wasted space it was before I bought it. Harriet? Might shed a tear or two, but I bet she'd be relieved to be rid of the family embarrassment.

My hands stopped moving and fell limply to the floor. I hung by my neck with my loose hair forming a curly halo as I stared at them. My ears roared as sound faded and my vision grayed. Dying this way didn't hurt. I expected it to, but it was more of a slow vanishing. I hoped Dodge would heal in time and find someone else to be with. Men like him deserved to be happy and loved.

A thump sounded, and I realized it was my head hitting the floor. A moment later, the cord was ripped from my throat, and I was rolled onto my back. My lungs didn't work. A mouth came down over mine and breathed for me, forcing air into my starved body. Again and again, someone breathed for me until I coughed and sputtered.

"She's back. Hand me the oxygen mask."

I heard screaming, thudding, begging, and crying

as a plastic cup covered my face. I tried to speak, but my throat hurt too damn bad.

Pain. I could feel pain.

I was still alive.

"Dodge, if you're gonna kill him, best not do it in front of me."

Blue. That was Betsey's son. My swollen eyes opened in tiny slits, and I saw Rafter's face above mine. I guessed he was the one who revived me.

"Don't try to speak yet. We got here in time, but you've got some damage. Ambulance is on the way." He glanced over to his left. "We're gonna need two before long. Dodge just beat the shit outta the guy who assaulted you. Your vitals are good, and I'd recommend staying awake, but if you want to pass out, that's okay. I'll keep you safe."

Passing out sounded like a handy-dandy-candy idea.

CHAPTER 34

I woke up in a hospital emergency room partition. Dodge was sitting in a chair next to me, his hand on mine. An IV bag hung above my head, and there were patches on my chest to measure my heartbeat. He noticed I was awake and stood to lean over me. His eyes were red.

"Fauna? Sweetness? Can you hear me?"

It hurt to move, so I blinked lazily and grunted a weird "Uh-huh" at him. My eyes moved to the Styrofoam pitcher on the table next to him.

"Water?" he asked.

At my gargling response, he poured a cup and placed a bendy straw to my lips. I sucked at the cool liquid and let it play over my tongue before attempting to swallow. It was tough and hurt like hell, but it worked.

"I called Macie, and he's on his way. Dewey's in jail. I haven't been charged with assault and battery, but that might be comin'. Blue is keepin' that off me right now." He stroked the curls back from the braids Tambre put in and maintained for me. "The doctor said you're gonna be fine in a few days. You've got some bad swelling and bruising, but he's got something going in the IV to help with that. I hope you don't mind, but I lied about our relationship and said we were married so I could give consent to take some blood for testing. Blue said if we can confirm GHB in your system, that's all the evidence needed to convict the fucker. They're also testing for DNA and are gonna try to get him for Zelda and Katie Grace too."

Tears overflowed his lower lids and tracked down his face. "If you hadn't started breathing again…."

He let the sentence drop.

I motioned him close and whispered in his ear, "Please don't fuck up Rafter for kissing me."

He laughed and brushed away the moisture from his cheeks. "No promises for any future contact, but I'll give him a pass this time. He will forever have my gratitude for saving your life."

A nurse came in and checked the IV bag, took my pulse, and made notes on a fancy rolling computer station. "The doctor said after you finish this, you can go home."

Home. The apartment? Nope. I'd rather have my bottom lip pulled over my head like a hat than go back there.

Dodge read my mind.

"We're going to the Lair. I'd prefer taking you to my room, but Betsey is insisting you stay upstairs in the guest suite where you were before. I wouldn't argue. You know who will win."

It took some time, but we arrived at the Lair sometime late in the afternoon. I felt like a steam-roller had run over me, backed up, and took a second turn. Prep at the restaurant hadn't been done, and I was panicking. How long would it take for me to recover enough to go back to work?

Dodge, in that uncanny way of his, answered that question.

"Macie wants to see you badly, but I told him to call after service tonight and see if you were still up. He and Katie Grace can handle the restaurant, and the other two chefs can cover temporarily. Betsey said she'd fill in or send her guys from the River's Edge to assist where needed. We got this covered, sweetness."

His kiss was affirming.

I did not like the idea of people coming to my restaurant and eating someone else's food, even if it was my recipe, but I wasn't stupid enough to think I could bounce out of this bed and hop down to my place.

Tears started flowing from my eyes. Fuck me, I hated crying, but I couldn't stop. It hit me how close I came to dying, probably within seconds. Those few moments when I lay helpless on the floor in my janky apartment. Alone. My breath gone. No way to fight back for the life I wanted so bad and had within my grasp. So much of my existence wasted on a family that couldn't care less about me, and just when I had a chance for one, to have it ripped away by a man I'd tried to accept as a friend.

The unfairness of it blended with sprinkles of outrage and a healthy dollop of fear on top. I was angry and scared. I wanted to both scream my rage and cower in the corner for protection at the same time. How dare someone do this to me? Try to end my life like I didn't matter? I *did* matter. I was not a second-class citizen because of my DNA, nor unworthy of this world, and I was so goddamn sick of trying to prove it.

Dodge leaned in closer and held my hand as he awkwardly bent to give me a full-body hug in the hospital bed. "I'm here, baby. I'll always be by your side no matter what, and we're gonna get through this shit together. You remember what I told you the first time we met?"

A picture of him straddling his bike came to me. He'd tapped the dragon symbol on the vest he wore. *"You see this patch? This means I'm a member of the Dragon Runners Motorcycle Club. We have a strong brotherhood tighter than any blood family and an unbreakable code of ethics. Any man who earns the right to wear this cut is one you can trust with your life."*

This man would always stand between me and danger. He would stay devoted to me for all our years to come, and when our kids were born, he would be an awesome father with unconditional love that had no limits. It was overwhelming and humbling.

"I love you, Dodge." My words were inadequate for all I experienced in those moments.

"I love you, too, Fauna."

I hoped I never took that love for granted.

EPILOGUE

After Dodge brought me to the Lair, Betsey fussed over me for days. Eva came to see me with her daughters. Lori came by with her newborn son. Kat went into labor, or otherwise she would have been there too. Psalm sent over a basket of lotions and soaps that filled my temporary quarters with fresh scents. Tambre came and did my hair. More people than I'd ever had in my life pampered and cared for me.

I didn't bother to inform Harriet or her family. I had my own.

On the third day of my convalescence, I was ready to leave the Lair and get back to work. I wasn't sure where I would go, but it wasn't back to that apartment. I'd turn that spot into a storage area rather than live there again. Dodge took care of that, too, and drove me to a cute little house not too far from the center of town. Three bedrooms, two baths, and a small, fenced yard. Brick had loaned him the down payment, and when Dodge sold either the Goat or the Ghia, he'd pay the club back.

A week after I went back to work, Dodge came in the restaurant after a day of "helping" his father. His face was solemn. Mallory had quietly passed away that morning. The alcohol in her system hadn't been a lethal level, but her organs couldn't cope after the abuse they'd suffered for so many years. They failed one by one without her ever regaining consciousness. There was still no way of knowing if she was one of Dewey's victims, but I wasn't sure it mattered. She was gone, and Dodge would mourn her despite their rocky lives.

Dewey was sitting in a prison somewhere waiting for his trial. He'd called Macie a few times, and even though that ship had sailed way off into the sunset, he had several revealing conversations with the man. According to Dewey, his family never fully accepted his homosexuality. They simply ignored it most of the time and referred to it as a phase he would eventually get out of his system. Somehow, Dewey became convinced that if he forced himself to have sex with women, he would stop being gay and his family would love him again. This didn't go very well, and he started drugging women to accomplish this task.

Obviously, it didn't work. The more he tried, the worse he felt. He confessed to drugging me that time at the Omni as his first attempt, but Dodge interfered with his plans that night. He'd been refining his technique and experimenting with doses and methods. Some of the other women, he could only mess with and not actually rape. Zelda was an accident. Katie Grace was supposed to be the one to finally free him, but he didn't expect her to be affected so quickly and publicly. After she fell down, something in his brain broke, and he decided the whole problem rested with me. I was the one who got away, and he needed to finish what he'd started. Immediately after his arrest, he tried to kill himself in his jail cell and ended up in a prison hospital. The latest news said he was in a psych ward and not doing well.

I can't help but wonder if he was so fucked-up between his family and his love for Macie that he had a really bad psychotic break or simply wanted to be caught. Even though the guy tried to strangle the life out of me, I kinda pitied him. Part of me hoped he would find his peace and heal from his own personal trauma.

Another part of me hoped he would choke on a big prison dick. He did attempt to kill me, after all.

Dodge's father made a surprise appearance at the hospital before I checked out. Dodge had gone to the garage to make an attempt at catching up on the backlog of work that had built up. I was fine with that, as I was champing at the bit to get away from the antiseptic-smelling place. An older man knocked on the door and came in when I called out permission.

He moved like he was ready to bolt at any moment. "You Fauna?" he asked.

I answered in the affirmative, wondering who he was and why he was there.

"I'm Boyer Plott. Dodge is my son."

"Okay." *Fuck me, what do I say now?* "Nice to meet you."

He mumbled something back, then fell silent. Awkward didn't come close to describing how uncomfortable that was.

"Umm… can I help you with something, Mr. Plott?"

"I understand you have a restaurant."

"Yes, the Smoky Mountain Bistro is mine. I'll treat you to meal if you come sometime."

"That chicken parm stuff you sent me was real good." The man wouldn't look me in the eye. His gaze darted from the floor to the wall and back.

"Thank you. I'm glad you liked it."

Quiet ensued again. I racked my brain to find something to say, some sort of common ground, but nothing came to my mind.

"Take care of my boy." He turned and left.

I told Dodge about the strange encounter, and to my surprise, my beautiful biker teared up.

"My dad doesn't leave the property for anything other than work. For him to come here means something, sweetness. It means a lot."

I pondered my life now as I placed a big platter of spanakopita triangles in the middle of a huge spread of food. The Dragon Runners' big Halloween barbecue was in full swing at their campground, and Betsey definitely ruled this roost. The walls of a big blue bouncy house flopped around, people were playing games, music boomed from Stud's band, and craft vendors hawked their wares. It was one big-ass block party, and I loved it.

Dodge was giving people rides on the Tail. He told me the final run would happen this evening, with all the club colors waving and all the bikers' old ladies at their backs.

I smiled. "I suppose that includes me."

He grinned and popped a triangle in his mouth. Brick had already eaten six or seven of them before he realized the stuff in the middle was spinach. "Yup. But you need something before we go."

"What's that?"

He pulled a box from his bike saddlebag. "Your own cut."

In the box was a black leather vest with a newly stitched Dragon Runners logo on the back along with "Property of Dodge" and my name on the front. The word *property* didn't sit well with me, but I'd learned the meaning from Betsey and the other old ladies. It was the committed form of marriage in their world. An unbreakable bond for life. Many of them still had official marriages and licenses, but as long as I had the kind of love I saw between Brick and Betsey, Mute and Kat, Stud and Eva, and all the rest, I had no complaints.

I slipped on the cut and posed for Dodge's approval. "How does it look?"

He placed a hand over his chin as he inspected me. "Hmmm. Something is still missing." He snapped his fingers as his face lit up. "I got it."

He reached into his pocket and pulled out a small box. My heart thumped.

"How 'bout spending a lifetime with me?"

I burst into laughter so I wouldn't cry. "I'm gonna need some wine to go with that cheese, baby. Put a ring on it and let's go for a ride."

ACKNOWLEDGMENTS

What an incredible journey, coming back to the mountains of North Carolina and the world of the Dragon Runners MC. I truly thought I was done with this series, but something whispered to me that there was more to the story. I owe a big part of that inspiration to Sharneisha Joyner, a former student of mine who is making waves in the world of music composition for video games and film. The other is Kania Mills, a good friend and colleague who has fought for and won her place as a performing clarinetist in North Carolina. I'm proud to call both of these women friends.

So much appreciation for everyone who helped get this book published. It's been a real challenge in many ways. Thanks to Kristin Scearce for putting up with my questions and for her attention to detail. Love to my beta readers, Jamee Thumm, Andrea Robinson, and Kim Deister. Your comments and critiques help keep me on track, which can be a full-time job. I can't thank Becky Johnson and the crew at

Hot Tree Publishing enough for continuing to walk this author road with me.

ABOUT THE AUTHOR

ML Nystrom has had stories in her head since she was a child. All sorts of stories of fantasy, romance, mystery, and anything else that captured her interest. A voracious reader, she's spent many hours devouring books; therefore, she found it only fitting she should write a few herself!

ML has spent most of her life as a performing musician and band instrument repair technician, but that doesn't mean she's pigeonholed into one mold. She's been a university professor, belly dancer, craftsperson, soap maker, singer, rock band artist, jewelry maker, lifeguard, swim coach, and whatever else she felt like exploring. As one of her students said to her once, "Life's too short to ignore the opportunities." She has no intention of ever stopping… so welcome to her story world. She hopes you enjoy it!

JOIN MY NEWSLETTER: HTTPS://WWW.MLNYSTROM.COM/ CONTACT

VISIT MY WEBSITE FOR MY CURRENT BOOKLIST: HTTPS://WWW.MLNYSTROM.COM/

ABOUT THE PUBLISHER

Hot Tree Publishing loves love. Publishing adult romantic fiction, HTPubs are all about diverse reads featuring heroes and heroines to swoon over. Since opening in 2015, HTPubs have published more than 300 titles across the wide and diverse range of romantic genres. If you're chasing a happily ever after in your favourite subgenre, HTPubs have you covered.

Interested in discovering more amazing reads brought to you by Hot Tree Publishing? Head over to the website for information:

WWW.HOTTREEPUBLISHING.COM

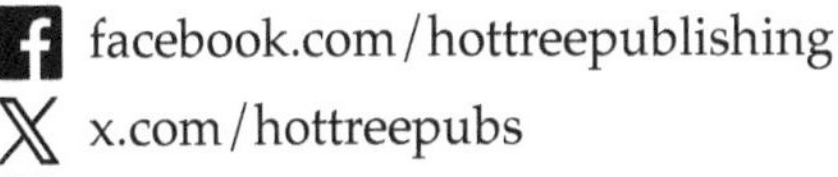

facebook.com/hottreepublishing
x.com/hottreepubs
instagram.com/hottreepublishing

www.ingramcontent.com/pod-product-compliance
Lightning Source LLC
Chambersburg PA
CBHW051238210726
48287CB00002B/293